I, POLYPHEMUS

Ron Terranova

Readlips Press

Editors: Della Rey & Jack Odman.

Art Direction: SunBow Productions

Cover Art: Matthew J. Price

Many thanks to our interns!

ISBN: 978-0-9990584-9-7

DEDICATION

This book is dedicated to Gerald Locklin-
Stand up poet
Stand up teacher
Stand up man.

I, POLYPHEMUS

Ron Terranova

CHAPTER I

I, Polyphemus, am a cyclops.

My gigantic size, my hirsute body, my feral smell and bent posture inspire fear and repulsion.

And then there is the matter of my singular eye.

It is disproportionately large and centered in the middle of my forehead. Far beyond my size and bestial demeanor, it is the single most terrifying and disconcerting feature for those who have never beheld a cyclops; those men – those mortals who behold with two eyes.

Those who have two eyes perceive the world through glassy orbs that are never truly in sync and harmony. One eye is always more dominant and focused than the other, hence, there is ambiguity and division in perception. Is the color they see blue, or, upon reflection, is it purple? Is the enemy far away, or perhaps depth perception is clouded and the enemy is within striking distance.

And then, of course, the matter of beauty.

Is she beautiful – truly beautiful? Perhaps at first glance, but a slight change in angle or vantage point may render her less so. We who have one centered eye know no such vacillating subjectivity. We see, unencumbered by ambiguity. We see reality with one singular vision. We see – without doubt or reservation. We see what is there.

CHAPTER II

You men. You mortal men who believe you know torment and suffering; desperation and loneliness. You think you know, with your civilization and your poetry – your science and your art. You know so little, in your world of light and hope.

You men who have inflicted me with anguish surpassing the anguish contained in all of Hades; who have punished me beyond the scope of the Fates and the furies – beyond the vengeance of the gods themselves – listen now. Listen to my story. Listen to the lament of the cyclops, Polyphemus.

CHAPTER III

The first absurd lash was my birth. My father, Poseidon, was one of a triumvirate of the most powerful of the gods. He was lord and master of all the sprawling seas and all of the creatures above and below their surface.

The other two were his brothers, Zeus and Hades. Hades ruled the shadowy underworld inhabited by the dead, and Zeus was the supreme ruler, lord of the sky and the infinite heavens. My father believed he was cheated by the Fates and that he was the legitimate supreme deity, not the pretender Zeus. You men, with your pitiful conflicts with your brethren. Imagine sibling rivalry on a cosmic scale; with the resulting tumult spilling onto the frail lives of mortals. Perhaps there is good in all of this, forging a balance of power, for indeed three wrathful gods at frequent odds with one another pose a better lot for men than one wrathful god unchecked and unbridled.

My mother was named Thoosa, a sea nymph of overwhelming beauty, or so I have been told. I really have no memory of her, as she severed the umbilical cord with urgent haste.

My parents - four wonderful eyes between them, and I was born with one, hideous to behold. A cyclops.

From the moment of my conception – before the beginning of sentience and cognition – I knew I was a monster.

It has been said that of all instincts, noble and base, no other is more powerful and benevolent than the instinct of maternalism. But with all truisms that attain the status of aphorism, there are exceptions.

I should have erupted from the womb a creature of blinding beauty and awesome power. Did not Pallas Athena erupt from the head of her father Zeus, magnificent and glorious, fully actualized at birth? Should I not too have been born, if not as a god, at least more than a grotesque thing?

But I came to this absurd world malformed and ponderous; immense, asymmetrical and flailing wildly at my rough exit from that warm, secure haven within my mother's belly. She was nearly torn asunder. They say she screamed, from the laceration of my birth, but louder yet and more horrifyingly when she stared into my monstrous eye.

Why would a union between a powerful god and a beautiful nymph result in a hideous one-eyed monster? For some things, even the gods have no control – except for one – Chaos.

Chaos – perhaps he was my true father, although he was not truly a god, but a formless state of being filling the void with darkness and confusion. Before there were gods, before there was night and nothingness, there was Chaos, and somehow his cold, colorless blood runs through my veins. Oh, but to have been spawned not by flesh but by a whirl of the irrational, to discover that Poseidon and Thoosa were fools and cuckolds – what satisfaction that would provide. But alas, these are feeble thoughts, like the reveries of the mad and the damned.

Given my lineage, had I been a reflection of my parents, my childhood undoubtedly would have been one of ease and privilege. But alas.

When one is despised by one's own parents – the parents who are among the elite of the higher beings – it is simple and natural for lesser beings to follow suit.

I have always pondered how many progeny my father has sired. Was he as prolific as his stronger brother Zeus, who could copulate with any desired female - goddess, nymph or mortal, at will and with absolute impunity? The poor, earnest and honest farmer, or herder, or stonecutter – what recourse would such a man have if his wife or daughter were violated by an omnipotent god? The gods are beyond compunction and morality, and can sate their lustful impulses without pause or consideration. Given that, the number of my siblings may be legion. Are there perhaps others like me, or am I an aberration, the mutant freak of the family?

I say I have no memory of my mother, but that is self-deception. My memory of her is porous and selective. I remember her beautiful face and the casual voluptuousness of her body, ripe and sensuous. I remember as if from a dream filled with mist and shadows. But alas, there is no memory within this dream of her coaxing language out of my cooing sounds, nor of cuddling and embraces and caresses. And of course there is no memory, within or without my dreams, of the nurturing sustenance of my mother's breast. None whatsoever.

But an infant cyclops, like any other, cannot fend for himself and requires food in the form of mother's milk. How was I suckled, you may ask, when my own mother was repulsed by her infant son?

There are stories and rumors about me which I can neither prove nor disprove. One story is that I was placed among the infant sheep who sustained life from the teats of a large, strong ewe.

Monster that I am, if the tale is true, I experienced love and acceptance for the first time from creatures meek and innocent, that saw me not as an object of disgust, but as one of their own. These gentle beings were my true family.

CHAPTER IV

My childhood was one of isolation. My peers, the other young cyclopes, did not know what to make of me. They were born of other cyclopes, but my own lineage was suspect. I intend no immodesty when I say I was superior to them. My strength and intellect far exceeded theirs, and they hated me for it; and feared me as well.

Once as we played in a large pasture (I alone; the others in small groups) a flock of nearby grazing sheep became agitated, then stricken by panic. I approached them to ascertain the source of their distress.

A large pack of wolves had emerged from the woods and began to stalk the sheep. Some began to cry, like children facing an unknown dread.

The other young cyclopes ran away from the danger, back to their homes.

I had no home.

I walked closer, placing myself between the sheep and the wolves. There were a dozen of them poised for the slaughter. A dozen predators set to attack sheep – oh, what a portending omen.

The leader of the pack looked up at me, his fangs like daggers, hatred burning in his eyes, ancient and without fear.

The other wolves moved outward with slow stealth toward my flanks. I knew by instinct I must not be encircled. I moved quickly.

My arm darted downward and I grabbed the leader by the scruff of his neck. He flailed and yelped loudly as I crushed and twisted his spine. Then he was still.

The others in the pack froze, giving me the time to grab the wolf corpse in my hand by his tail. And then, like a farmer wielding a scythe, I swung my lupine club back and forth at the remaining pack. I moved with a frenzy.

It was almost comical as wolf bodies careened in the air bouncing off trees and twirling from my club's impact like acrobats at a fair. A few that were neither dead nor maimed took flight into the woods.

I looked upon the sheep. Slowly, they regained their composure.

Oh, how they appeared to me. So soft, and sweetly innocent.

CHAPTER V

As I grew, I began to accept. I would never be embraced by my own kind. The reality was, there were none of my own kind – not truly. No, I would never be a part of a greater whole. I was the other in a world of others.

As I reached adolescence, I began to notice changes within and without. Often, I would see my cyclopes brothers and sisters, communing with one another in groups, at work and in play. It was different from before. Now the sexes co-mingled, and there would be laughter punctuating their activities. I rarely played, and I worked alone.

They bonded within their tight units. Periodically, they would pause in their pursuits, and stare, like birds in unison at some stimulus; some external aberration that evoked fear or curiosity; then, return herd-like, to their activities.

When they would see me, however, the pause was different. They would stop their endeavors and gawk in puzzlement. Was I truly a cyclops, a member of the race and tribe, or something else? Was I in fact a freakish hybrid – not quite cyclops, but an unholy blend of deity, human and cloven hooved animal?

When one defies definition, one is an outcast and pariah. Ah, to be examined and judged by a collection of single eyes connected to minds that in their numbers were inferior to my own. Isolated and cast apart was my lot, per the pleasure of the bitch Fates.

And so be it. If I was not destined to receive their love, then I would receive their respect by being feared.

CHAPTER VI

One day, in mid-spring, I was in the woods, sitting upon a stone by a brook. Even in a world of strife and turmoil, there are nooks and niches where one can find peace and tranquility. But in the world in which I live, peace and tranquility are ephemeral.

I listened to the sounds of the woods; the calming sound of the breeze and the soft babble from the brook when all of a sudden I heard music.

It was flute music. Strange flute music, at turns both soothing and provocative. Such an otherworldly sound, permeating through the forest as dusk approached and the trees danced and fanned the warm air.

It was mesmerizing. It was almost as if the music was coming from the dark green thicket of the trees itself, independent of flute or flautist.

As I listened, the sweet melodies swirled inside my head, seductive and sensual.

My body felt light and buoyant, and to my incredulity I arose and began to dance. A cyclops dancing! I may very well have set a precedent, for among the race of cyclops, terpsichorean we are not.

It was exhilarating – no other music had ever had this effect on me before. My will and control were slaves to the magic sound.

Then, abruptly, it stopped and I heard a voice.

"Even the gods envy my flute playing virtuosity, if I say so myself."

A figure stepped into the clearing. And my, what a strange figure it was.

I had heard of satyrs, but had never actually seen one.

He was as tall as a man, but his human characteristics were adulterated. He bore the hindquarters, legs and hooves of a goat. And atop his head were thick, powerful horns, more stag-like than goat. And beneath his loincloth was a male endowment that seemed almost comical by its abundance.

"Allow me to introduce myself." His statement was punctuated with a brief riff on his flute. "My name is Pan."

Pan. I had heard of him since early childhood, but never truly believed he existed. Pan, the frolicsome, mischievous god of all the wild and wooded places in the world. Pan, the patron and protector of goat herders, and the irresistible seducer of nymphs of the woodland.

And, held to his lips, the flute was mightier than the sword.

"And who, young lad, are you? And why are you so forlorn? You should be merry and carefree. Dusk is near and the moon is full. Soon, the woods will rumble with the flow of wine and the dancing of nymphs."

I looked upon this strange and merry goat man. Even a cyclops would appear attractive compared to him. And yet, his power and magnetism were apparent. He was king of the woods and his flute was his scepter.

"My name, sir, is Polyphemus. And pardon me if I appear to be staring. I am a cyclops, and I always appear to be staring."

He broke into a gaping smile and walked closer to me. His gait was jaunty as his goat hooves broke the twigs on the forest floor. The crackling sounds from his steps made the forest sound as if it were on fire.

"Of course – a cyclops! And an excellent specimen of one, if I may be so impertinent to comment." His eyes raked my body, from top to bottom. A crimson blush came to my face.

"I have known a few cyclopes in my time," he continued. "A very special breed they are – very special indeed. Large muscular specimens, like yourself. Excellent shepherds and wine makers. A bit solitary and taciturn, perhaps. All of you – you in particular I would venture – need to get out more and have some fun. Be open-minded and stop focusing on the dark, ill-tempered gods. We who revel and worship within the woods pray to the Lord Dionysus, and we are rewarded with joy and ecstasy."

Such a merry proselytizer, I thought. If he looked more like Adonis, and less like a goat, he could be a superb leader.

I could not help, however, but to consider his words.

I had been an insular, darkly pessimistic creature all of my life. I had assumed my outlook was due to circumstance, but perhaps that only exacerbated my inherent nature. I had seen some meager display of joy and exuberance within the fraternity of cyclopes, but compared to the nymphs and satyrs we were like oarsman rowing across the river Styx.

Pan's eyes widened and sparkled. "Listen," he exhorted, "Listen to the forest, Polyphemus. Do you hear? They are on their way and will be here soon."

"Who," I implored. "Who will be here soon?"

"The Maenads – the wild women of the woods. They have been driven mad by the wine of Dionysus. They will tear every living creature in their path limb from limb and devour their flesh with appetites insatiable. Even a mighty cyclops like yourself will be overwhelmed, your bones will be picked clean. Unless…"

I listened as he spoke. The trees begin to rattle and a shrill, keening sound pierced the woods. The sound increased in intensity and I felt a chilled tingle at the base of my spine.

Then, they appeared in the clearing.

They were young, lithe and voluptuous, and their eyes were afire with madness. They wore white, diaphanous robes which were tattered by their chaotic rampage through the forest, and wreaths of twisted branches decorated their hair. As they keened they waved wands in the air, wands tipped with pinecones shaped to resemble skulls. Dancing in place, they stomped their feet and in unison they pointed their sinister wands toward me. The pitch of their screech heightened, and I was about to cover my ears when the entire deranged horde darted toward me.

I looked about, frantic as they closed in. Had they been stout male warriors my terror would have been less. There was a rage and fury in their faces that transcended hate and irrationality.

Just before they were upon me, Pan withdrew his flute from his belt and began to play.

They stopped in their tracks.

The music floated over the Maenads then descended, like a hypnotic vapor coursing through their ears. Their frenzy was stilled, and their crazed countenance and demeanor became tranquil.

Drawing their hands together is if in prayer, they raised their arms over their heads and began to sway as they looked upward toward the heavens.

The dread I had felt a moment ago was gone. I too felt the hypnotic effect of Pan's magical flute.

I felt calm – almost sedated – and yet energized. I looked about the woods. The leaves and branches of the trees wriggled in the soft wind and seemed to gesture in sly flirtation.

Pan had now changed the tempo of his playing. The notes were higher and the rhythms faster.

The Maenads clasped one another's hands and begin a child-like dance around me. They giggled as they swirled, their whirling pace increasing to keep up with the frenetic music of Pan's flute. Around and around they went, faster and faster until their individual shapes blended into a white blur.

I looked toward Pan. His fingers moved across his flute with dizzying speed and his lips pulsated like a dying star.

Faster and faster the Maenads whipped around me, until the air grew hot and the whirling circle began to emit sparks.

Then, there was a thunderous crack and a banshee scream, and the Maenads were gone, up in smoke without a trace.

Pan swaggered toward me, not even attempting to conceal his smug satisfaction.

"Well, my dear boy, I have been subjected to all manner of insult and criticism in my time, but no one – not Zeus himself, ever said I was not a flautist!"

I looked about. The forest had reclaimed normality. Had I imagined it all?

"Bend forward, Polyphemus, so I may reach your head."

It seemed inappropriate under the circumstances not to comply.

I bowed deeply, and, gently, Pan tapped my head with his flute.

"There my boy. I have bestowed a gift upon you. Your self-esteem is dangerously low and you have no confidence with the fairer sex. Through the power of my flute I have granted you seductive charm and savoir-faire. Enough so that even a nymph – the most beautiful of nymphs – would find you irresistible. Now, go forth, and ply your charms on the sisterhood of nymphs."

He turned from me to disappear back into the woods. Then he turned around and looked me in the eye and exhorted –

"But do not try to charm the Maenads – in the name of sweet Hades, keep away from the Maenads!"

CHAPTER VII

It did not take long for the magic to work.

I was walking in the woods, pensive and solitary, when I saw her. The vision of her was an awakening; an awakening of such intensity it was as if I had been born blind and could suddenly see for the first time.

One eye, one vision. She possessed my perception. There was really nothing else to see but her.

I approached her slowly as she was bathing in the tree-shaded stream. The sunlight wove through the forest branches, illuminating her in golden brilliance.

I was transformed. I felt a lightness, a release of burdensome weight from my shoulders.

I was reborn.

Pausing in the stream, my beautiful nymph looked up and stared directly at me.

My heart dropped. Blessed by Pan or not, I was a cyclops – surely she would flee in dread and repulsion.

But she did not. She stared deeply into my eye, and smiled. Then, she reached out and touched me.

"Hello," she said. "My name is Galatea."

All of my life I had felt unclean and disgusting. Then Galatea, the sea nymph, touched me.

We began to talk. I had always been awkward and withdrawn in conversation, whether with fellow cyclopes or mortals. But my inhibitions were gone, and I smiled as we conversed. *Pan you sly old satyr!* The magic from his flute coursed through me and words flowed from my mouth as if scripted by the great poets.

Oh, how beautiful she was when she laughed. Was she under a spell?

How could this be so? How could a female of such sublime beauty not see me for what I am? Or perhaps it was I, beaten and shunned, who never saw myself as I could be.

We began to meet daily by the stream. We would talk for hours. My beautiful, coquettish sea nymph. Once, when she stood up from the stream, her robe clung to her, as if the fabric's fibers were attempting to enter her pores. I nearly toppled from the lightheadedness. She would listen with compassion as I told her of my life, at times holding my head to her breast; or, she could be playfully mocking. Galatea, with her endless tresses of red hair and her alabaster skin. Her complexion – as white as the milk of lambs, her eyes, as green as an emerald sea.

My life had never known such joy. She was my temptress and my salvation. An enticing sprite, who was less and more than mortal, as am I.

She would appear, sometimes from the corner of my eye, then suddenly disappear. Was she real, or an apparition, wed to the springs and ponds that pocketed the forest?

On one warm day when the sun pulsed red and loomed in the sky, she emerged from her stream, naked and bold. She took me by the hand and led me to a meadow. Then she laid me down on my back on the velvety grass.

Slowly, she straddled my loins, kissing my chest and face. "Slowly – slowly so as not to hurt me, my beautiful giant."

I had never been loved before. Galatea loved me on that beautiful day.

At some point I expected recoil, but there was none. She held her head on my chest, listening to my heart as we rested.

"Polyphemus – the fierce, one-eyed brute who terrorizes both man and beast. The unapproachable monster feared by all – except me. I never believed what they said about you. Lies – all lies."

She moved her face close to mine. The gentle breeze spread the sweetness of her breath.

"But I have never been afraid." There was a tender mischief in her eyes; those green eyes, green as the mysteries of the forest. Her lips moved to my ear and she whispered. "I have never been afraid because I know a secret – I know *your* secret."

I could not help but to stiffen at her words. Where was she going with this – what did she know?

"You have a secret," she continued. "A secret you have kept to yourself all of your life. A secret you cling to as if your life depended on it."

I felt like placing my hand over her mouth, to quiet her, to suffocate the words before they could be spoken. But my hand froze with the same chill that ran the length of my spine.

"I have watched you. You have entered into the vocation of shepherding. But you are different from other shepherds. For the others, the sheep are commodities to be shaved and slaughtered. But to you, they are something different. They are your children. And that you must conceal, because in our savage world the gentle are deemed weak. You, Polyphemus, are a gentle, caring father to your innocent children."

CHAPTER VIII

I, a father? Many males – mortal, god, cyclops – have treasured memories of their fathers. Let me tell you more about my father.

Yes, my father was a god. **Poseidon, lord and** ruler of the many seas, but that was not enough. My earlier description does him little justice. He was a jealous god, contemptuous of his brother Hades, and insane with hate for his brother Zeus.

Yes, my father believed he was the rightful ruler of every realm, be it ocean, earth, heaven or hell. But he was loathed by his own creator, Cronus, who held my father's brothers in greater favor. Ha! The redundancy of the bitch Fates. The despised son in due course becomes the hateful father.

Yes, my father despised me from the moment of my birth. Such a dismal reflection was I of his cosmic manhood. When he would ride his golden vessel across the seas, the waves would cower and the currents cease. His flaming hair billowed in the sky, lashing out at the sun and the heavens, whipping through the air inspiring thunderclaps and fiery bolts of lightning. The dolphins and the fish from the sea would jettison from the watery depths in synchronized homage to their lord and master as he raised his mighty trident in celebration of his power and majesty. Such a perfect, beautiful deity - such a wondrous site to behold.

And his son? Those with the misfortune to set sight of him quickly averted their eyes.

CHAPTER IX

Yes, my parents. Poseidon and Thoosa. One, a god; the other a sea nymph. One could summon thunderbolts from the heavens, and the other bolted from her hideous offspring.

Left to my own devices and to the kindness of strangers; the latter an oxymoron, I quickly learned.

CHAPTER X

There are stories deeply embedded in the collective psyche of men, and other thinking creatures, about infants who were orphaned or abandoned at birth. The most common denominator in these stories is the wolf. Abandoned and helpless, for some inexplicable reason, the doomed foundling is taken in by a species that would ordinarily recognize an easy, mouthwateringly tender meal, and follow instinct by devouring the tiny, hapless creature. But somehow, in special cases, these rapacious predators are overwhelmed by compassion and mercy, and are transformed into nurturing protectors. Or so go the tales.

The primary prey of wolves is sheep.

Somehow in my case, sheep in wolves' clothing discovered me and became my saviors.

Or so goes the tale.

Sheep, through the ages, have been misconstrued. They are seen as passive, docile creatures, physically weak and mentally feeble; easily led, and unresistant to slaughter. Ah, so easy to accept this stereotype. I would suggest that you, oh gentle reader, are so lockstep in accepting this stereotype that you are, ironically, sheep like.

Sheep are strong and good but have been cursed by the gods. In the state of nature, those creatures possessing claws have an advantage – those with hands are most advantaged of all. Sheep have been cursed with hooves, which are ill suited to both craft and combat.

But rams, with their formidable horns and fierce dispositions, are creatures with which to be reckoned when their families are threatened. And ewes, as gentle as they appear, are powerful in their maternalism. They will instinctively put themselves between danger and their offspring.

Yes, the more I reflect, the evidence that I was raised by sheep is compelling.

I have known sheep, and I have known men, and what have I concluded? Most sheep are better men than most men. Sheep are summarily led off to slaughter by men.

Better to slaughter a man than a sheep.

CHAPTER XI

It was a day that began as many others. Dawn, and its sunlight broke through the tree line, forming beams, golden spokes, beautiful and warm.

I awoke, feeling young and hopeful. The world changes when one is in love – or so it seems. Sounds, ordinary or obnoxious, become melodic. Smells, pungent and odiferous, become aromatic. All things, benign or bad, become good.

Love can also intoxicate and beguile. Oh, my beloved Galatea. I set out to find her, taking the trail that led to her favorite stream. As I walked, monarch butterflies blanketed my path, darting and swirling about. There was magic all about as I trekked toward the one I loved.

And when I arrived at the stream, I saw her. She was happier and more alive than I had ever seen her. But she was not alone. She was with another. She was with Acis.

CHAPTER XII

He was the proverbial handsome prince. His long, curly locks fell to his shoulders, golden and thick. He was tall – for a man – and well-muscled. The sinews in his chest swelled and writhed, as he and Galatea played in the shallow water; they played and caressed amidst their joy and laughter, the way only lovers can. I gaped, my eye wide and on fire. The wind had been knocked out of me, and my soul went with it. I struggled to breathe. I could not help but to watch them. He was caressing her breasts.

I approached them with numb stealth. The sound of their laughter became louder as I grew near. Then, they saw me. The laughter stopped.

Galatea was dumbstruck, but her precious lover – her arrogant little prince, looked upon me with no fear. I must have appeared to him as a dumb, harmless brute. He was confident from a lifetime of privilege and entitlement. All of his battles in life had been settled by others beneath his station.

He could have sport with me with absolute impunity – or so he thought.

He smiled graciously, then spoke.

"Well – who do we have here? Who is this hirsute, malodorous creature, who graces our presence? Could it be Polyphemus? Galatea has spoken of you often. But sadly, she speaks with disgusted gags and contemptuous titters, never providing an adequate description – alas, my pre-conception of you was never fully realized; until now. Oh, what an enormously grotesque, one-eyed clown you are!"

"Polyphemus," Galatea shrieked. "Do not believe him – he lies! Yes, he is my lover, but that does not mean I had no love for you."

She spoke, but I did not hear her. Her words were dead and hollow. But Acis's words hung in the air like fixtures fastened to the space separating us.

My mood changed. I smiled.

With one hand, I grabbed the fair prince by his flowing locks deep at the roots and lifted. It seemed the trees swayed from the rush of his screams. He flailed and kicked, a doomed puppet dancing toward death.

I looked at her. I looked at the horror and awe in her eyes. She made no protest and showed no sympathy for her anguished lover. Ah, my beautiful Galatea; my radiant, heartless whore.

Turning my attention back to my hapless rival, with my free hand I bore down on his shoulder and lifted upward with my other hand. I pressed down, harder, until his body hit the ground.

His entire scalp was twisted in my bloody palm.

He stared up at me, eyes gaping in astonishment as his body convulsed. I could not resist. "I'm sorry, Prince Acis. What were you saying a moment ago? Was it something about my appearance?"

The end was quick and unceremonious. His head was crushed beyond recognition beneath my foot.

I was tempted to pound my chest in triumph, but I could almost hear Pan's admonition – "How vulgar; how woefully vulgar." Yes. One should attempt to preserve a degree of dignity after such a barbaric display.

And what of Galatea? And what of the disgusting mess I still held in my hand?

I turned and walked away from the former.

The latter was cleaned and dried and worn as a talisman around my belt.

My delusion had ended. Love is a figment, ephemeral, like smoke and dew. It is for men. I am not a man.

I am a cyclops.

CHAPTER XIII

Information flows slowly to one such as I, but in time I do hear of the happenings in the world.

And how does the information flow? There are messengers who travel far and wide, and often when they arrive their words are ancient and meaningless. Information travels more quickly through the medium of seers and soothsayers. And then, there are dreams.

Reports of the fall of Troy had spread with haste, even to my remote island. When news has import, Hermes is the messenger.

Details were sparse. There were rumors that the long stalemate of ten years was ended by a horse.

Priam, the wise king of the city state, proved to be a fool. He should have listened.

He should have listened – to his daughter, Cassandra.

She was blessed by Apollo himself with the gift of prophecy, or so rumors say. Others believed she was born with the gift. Gift? She knew better than anyone of the duplicity of gifts.

The horse. The immense horse.

Cassandra exhorted her father to reject the great horse, the gift from the Greeks – their homage to the mighty Trojans who had outlasted them.

"Beware," she screamed. "Beware of Greeks bearing gifts." But he scoffed, and met her warnings with rage.

He cast his own daughter, poor tragic Cassandra, out of the city.

Why do the greatest prophets have the darkest visions?

The horse was an equine engine of doom, containing Greeks who cast open the mighty gates of Troy as the Trojans slept after a day of drunken revelry in celebration of their victory. The city was sacked, and Cassandra was discovered by the Greeks, seeking refuge in the Temple of Athena.

She was defiled by the Greeks, who in turn raised the wrath of Athena.

Cassandra – guilty of seeing the truth; doomed for speaking of it.

The horse. The death horse. Who could devise such a lethal deceit?

Once in a dream I saw a man who was a warrior prince who loathed his comrades and despised the war to which he was forcibly conscripted. A man who yearned to be reunited with his family and to return home.

This man was the architect of the horse.

When one pleases one god, one is cursed by another.

And this, in my dream, this man was long suffering. And for this, I feel a bond, a connection, with this tormented wandering pawn of gods and furies.

Dreams. So many dreams. How do we know that all we experience is not a dream? Are we protected from the Fates within our dreams; do our dreams belong to us, or are they also woven by the bitch Fates?

Once, long ago as a boy, I had a dream.

I was drowning below the surface of a pond. I could not breathe and I could not scream. Then, from below and through frantic ripples, I saw her. The beautiful girl with tragic eyes. She reached down and pulled me to the surface. I closed my eye and breathed deeply – then she was gone.

CHAPTER XIX

For some men and monsters, after the first love there are no others. My love for Galatea was unrequited. What I thought was a connection with my soul mate was, in fact, a sojourn with a shallow, manipulative tease; a duplicitous tormentor of monsters such as I, and a guide to destruction for the easily charmed such as Acis.

My experience of love compelled me to be resigned – resigned to a life of isolation and distance from others of my own kind.

My own kind. I no longer know what that means.

CHAPTER XV

They are so warm and vulnerable when first born. Has there ever been a creature so innocent and pure as a lamb?

Has there ever been a creature so vile and destructive as a man?

If indeed I was nurtured and rescued from abandonment by sheep, then let me recede from this world of deceit and cruelty and live among them once again.

I must learn the trade of shepherding.

CHAPTER XVI

I believe one learns from observation.

I had developed a routine in which I would arise at dawn and from a distance watch shepherds tending sheep. Pan was correct. We cyclopes seem to have a knack for tending to sheep. For hours I would observe their techniques and behaviors.

One day on my way to a pasture, I saw a horse in a thicket of trees. I blinked. No – not a horse, but a man. I blinked again. No, it was a man mounted on a horse. Then, after blinking several more times, I realized what I was seeing.

It was a centaur.

CHAPTER XVII

My fascinated staring ended abruptly. The centaur turned his head toward me and bellowed, "You – yes you, young cyclops – stop your gawking!"

My mouth gaped and gasped. I had never encountered a centaur before. I had only heard stories. They were invariably depicted as gross, licentious creatures, crude in their ways and violent. It never occurred to me they could speak.

"So, I suppose you saw what I was doing?" the centaur continued.

"Doing? Why no, I did not see you doing anything," I replied. "But you did appear to be in a state of keen concentration."

"Ah, so you did see!" He punctuated his retort with a harsh stomp with his hoof upon the forest floor.

"No – no sir – I did not; I saw nothing."

"Well – well good," the centaur continued. "The fact is, I have not done it yet. So kindly turn your head – avert your eye, young cyclops, so I can do it."

I did as he requested. Then, after a period of minutes, he spoke again.

"There. There now. I am now in better sorts."

He strode toward me from the thicket and I got a better look at him. Yes, the body of a horse, but the arms, torso and head of a man. His upper body was that of a well-muscled youth, but his face was of an older, albeit handsome gentleman. His forehead was wide, his brows thick and his beard neatly trimmed. Ah, the extreme incongruity. It was as if the gods, in a state of boredom, amused themselves by stitching the upper half of a philosopher onto the lower half of a stallion.

"What is your name, young cyclops?"

"My name is Polyphemus."

"Well, young Polyphemus, my name is Chiron, and I can assure you I am nothing like the stampeding rabble of the others with whom I bear a resemblance. I am known as a creature of refinement and learning. I am versed in medicine and healing, as well as archery and the hunt. I am expert in music and poetry, as well as prophecy. You may not have heard of me, my isolated young cyclops, but I am renown and have often been solicited by the gods themselves to mentor their offspring."

He paused, then smiled with wry amusement.

"Have you any idea, my young cyclops, how mortifying it is for one of my dignity to defecate in the woods like horse?"

CHAPTER XVIII

This was not my last encounter with the centaur Chiron. We spoke at length that day, and he opined that my social isolation had left enormous gaps in my education. In exchange for an occasional goatskin of wine, he offered to mentor me in the many disciplines which he had mastered.

As the weather is usually moderate, we usually met in a secluded grove for my lessons.

We began with philosophy. Sitting comfortably beneath an oak (Chiron remained standing for various reasons, not the least of which was the inherent indignity of a centaur sitting on his haunches.)

"All right my boy – listen carefully." Chiron cleared his throat and shifted his shoulders, assuming a more professorial stature. "We are beginning with a lesson in philosophy for a reason, for indeed philosophy is the love of reason and of wisdom." He looked down at me as he cleared his throat again. There was a critical glint in his eyes. "Are you listening, young cyclops?"

"Yes – yes sir." And I was. But it was a beautiful day and distractions were everywhere.

Chiron continued. "Now, as you well know, my boy, we live in a world where events beget other events – a world of cause and effect. And because of this, the rational observer can examine phenomena, and draw logical conclusions about the nature of things, and how those things came to be. Would you agree with this postulate, my boy?"

I thought carefully, then answered, "Yes – yes Chiron, I would agree."

Again, he looked down at me. I sensed he was not entirely pleased with my answer. He continued.

"Now, as you well know my boy, we live in a world where the reasonable flow of events is influenced by the intervention of the gods, and what appears to be cause and effect is illusion; the nature of things is merely the result of the gods' caprice and whimsy. Would you agree with this postulate, my boy?"

I began to feel uncomfortable. I thought of the bitch Fates. I thought of my father.

"Yes – yes Chiron. I would agree."

Chiron's reaction was completely unexpected.

Making an absurd, whinnying sound through fluttering lips, he turned his hind side to me, then kicked grass and dirt into my face with his hind legs. Then, he regained his composure.

"You were not listening, young cyclops. You agreed to two diametrically opposed postulates. You exasperate me! And when I am exasperated, the equine half of my nature takes over, and it is… it is humiliating!"

A few moments passed, and Chiron was back to full professorial mode.

"Now, my boy, to continue."

I cordoned off the beautiful day and listened, as I have never listened before.

CHAPTER XIX

The lessons continued. Chiron's mentoring philosophy was that a diversity of disciplines should be taught on a revolving schedule.

It was day one of archery.

The lesson began with the proper technique of stringing the bow.

Chiron produced a beautifully carved, polished bow, which he handled with a finesse bordering on reverence.

"Look at this instrument, my boy – this work of art. It is the tool of the warrior and the hunter. It is a thing of destruction, and a thing of beauty. To string the bow is not an act of brute strength, but of applied leverage."

He raised the bow and pushed the ends. The bow bent in one direction, then suddenly turned within itself. The string was straight and taut.

"Now, Polyphemus, you try. And remember – finesse and leverage."

He handed me the bow. It looked absurdly small in my gigantic hands.

I tried to mimic Chiron's movements. Finesse and leverage, I thought. Finesse and leverage.

I pushed the ends together, and with a sickening crack the bow splintered into countless pieces.

Amidst the sound of disgusted whinnying and the sight of Chiron's backside, half the forest floor was kicked into my face.

CHAPTER XX

As an adjunct to my philosophy lessons, Chiron would at times engage me in the discipline of dialogue, but more often than not he would forego his usual pedantry and we would simply converse as friends (although he could not help but to remind me with various degrees of subtlety which friend was the wiser.)

It was a warm day in late spring as Chiron and I had one of our conversations. I sat beneath my favorite tree as Chiron, per custom, stood over me. (I could not conceive of him sitting, and, I imagined, he probably slept upright like a.... well, like a horse.) An acquired distaste for woodland turf prevented me from ever broaching this possibility with my learned mentor.

In true mentor/protégé protocol, Chiron initiated the discussion.

"So tell me, Polyphemus – do you believe in the existence of the gods?"

I began to fidget, sensing another display of equine disapproval upon an errant response.

"Oh, relax my boy. Both halves of me are jovial today, and indeed, there are no right or wrong answers. Relax, and talk with me as you would with an old friend who is your equal."

I took a deep breath, then answered.

"Yes, I do. If for no other reason than my father is a god. My father is Poseidon."

Chiron smiled, "Yes, yes – of course he is, my boy. What are your memories of him? What does he look like? When did you last see him?"

My mind reeled. I knew exactly what my father looked like. But when did I last see him?

"I can tell you what he looks like. Powerful, radiant – cruel. But I have not seen him since I was in infant."

"Ah, how very fascinating," Chiron replied. "Most adults have no memory of experiences from infancy. But of course if you are indeed the son of a great god, your memory may be more acute."

"I'm sure I've seen him. My memory is too vivid and detailed," I replied.

I looked at him. Did I detect the beginning of a flutter of his lips? I quickly expanded my answer.

"Well, it is generally accepted that Poseidon is my father. It… it has never been refuted or questioned."

Chiron was clearly not pleased with my answer. But he was true to his word and retained his composure.

"My boy, it has never been refuted that Poseidon is my father. Ah, the power of refutation. Can one logically infer because neither of us have been refuted as the sons of Poseidon, that, therefore, we are brothers?"

The temptation to blurt out "Chiron, you old horse!" was overwhelming, but I contained myself. My mind reeled. Then, I was struck by an answer.

"No, because no one has asserted that you are son to Poseidon or brother to Polyphemus."

He beamed with pride.

"Excellent my boy – excellent!"

CHAPTER XXI

From that point on, Chiron became far more of a friend and confidant than a stern professor.

I told him of my life and of my trials. I told him of loneliness and isolation, of love and betrayal.

And I told him of my sense of rage.

"It's always there, Chiron. Always, just below the surface, softly simmering or at full boil. Not that long ago I had fallen in love with a beautiful nymph named Galatea. She changed my world and I believed she loved me as well… and during that brief period the rage was gone."

I looked at Chiron. I looked into his kind, weary eyes. I began to choke.

"It's alright my boy, it's alright. You may stop if it's too painful. Perhaps another time."

"No, Chiron. I need to finish. I need to speak the words and release the burden." My brow trembled. I breathed deeply, then continued.

"But she never loved me. I am a cyclops; brutish and hideous to behold…"

"No, no, my boy," interrupted Chiron. "You are far more and far better than you believe. You are brave and powerful and intelligent. Hideous? Nonsense my boy – nonsense!"

He paused, then a spark of mischief appeared in his eyes.

"I have known a nymph or two in my time." He looked about, as if concerned there may be eavesdroppers. Then he winked conspiratorially and whispered, "We centaurs are actually much coveted within the nymph community. Try not to conjecture upon the mechanics, just except what I say. Oh, what sluts those nymphs be! And shallow! No creature on earth is a poorer judge of beauty than a nymph."

I could not help but to smile. Would Chiron continue his jocularity when I finished my lament?

"One day I found my love, Galatea, with a handsome young man. They had been making love. This young man was a prince. He was arrogant and cruel and spoke to me with a vicious disdain."

I needed to pause before confessing my sin.

"I killed him, Chiron. I tore off his scalp then crushed his head with my foot. And I feel neither guilt nor remorse."

Chiron reflected upon my words, then he gazed at my belt and raised an eyebrow.

"Tell me my boy – this handsome young prince you dispatched; was his name perchance Acis?"

I drew back, startled. "Yes – yes. How did you know?"

He looked again at my belt.

"How can one help but to notice the trophy you carry on your belt? The beautiful flaxen hair braided to the leathery scalp. That is the hair of Acis. Oh, how many lush nymphs have interrupted my dalliances in favor of young Acis? If given a gold coin for every time I wanted to gallop over his smug face I would be as rich as Midas."

I was dumbfounded. Was this truly Chiron speaking?

"Guilt – remorse? Oh my boy you are so harsh with yourself. Of course there should be no guilt or remorse. What you did is akin to an act of public service. That vain, vicious twit is gone. Do you realize what this means, young Polyphemus?"

Was this an act? Did he ask a trick question? How could he be so ecstatic over my act of homicide?

"No, Chiron. I have no answer. What does it mean?"

"It means there will be more available nymphs for centaurs and cyclopes. In that order. That's what it means."

Then, he roared with laughter, enough to frighten the forest fauna.

"This deserves a drink, my dear friend, Polyphemus."

Then, he looked upward to the heavens.

"Perhaps my sophistry was in error. Perhaps, Polyphemus, you and I truly are brothers!"

CHAPTER XXII

When I was not with Chiron for my lessons, I was preoccupied with learning a livelihood.

I continued observing shepherds plying their craft, and when I felt I understood the fundamentals, I approached several of them and worked as their assistant.

One day I approached a large, older cyclops. He was bent and used his staff as a cane. His name was Democulus.

"Good morning, sir. My name is Polyphemus, and I'm looking for work as a shepherd's assistant. I am strong and a hard worker, and will work in exchange for some of your milk and cheese." I extended my hand in friendship.

My gesture was ignored.

"My name is Democulus. I'm old and I feel my years. I can use help. But let me warn you, Polyphemus, I am ill-tempered, and I don't suffer fools lightly. If you're willing to work for food only, then you have a job. But you will work."

His eye narrowed giving him a serpentine appearance.

"Oh yes – you will work!"

CHAPTER XXIII

I met Democulus in the pasture at the dawn's earliest light. The sheep had already been herded when I arrived.

Democulus' self-description of being ill-tempered was a gross understatement. He would lean into his staff and jabber with an unpleasant incoherence. Every few minutes he would make disgusting gagging sounds, then spit sputum and bile at the sheep. During my apprenticeship I had observed that most shepherds are stern but gentle with their flocks, but this was not the case with Democulus. At the first sign of disorder or deviation from the flock, he would jab at the offending sheep with his staff. At times the staff would strike a lamb eliciting a cry of pain and fear. Democulus saw me wince.

"Wool, milk and mutton. That's all they are. I don't care what they feel. They were put here for one reason. Sheep. Ha! They were born to be shorn and slaughtered – shorn and slaughtered!"

I looked upon the cowering sheep. Then I looked at Democulus.

My blood began to simmer with hatred.

CHAPTER XXIV

I was tempted to spit in Democulus' eye and find work elsewhere, but the sheep kept me tethered to my post. How abusive did he get with his flock? I had known others like him. There are cyclopes, just as there are men and gods, for whom cruelty is not a means to an end but is the end. Perhaps, I hoped, if I could not change Democulus' nature I could at least act as a buffer between him and the flock.

One morning he approached me and stated that to better contain the sheep a corral needed to be built.

There was a quarry some distance from the pasture area. Democulus did indeed expect me to work.

"You are young and strong, Polyphemus; perhaps stronger than any cyclops I have known. Put your youth and strength to good use and go to the quarry. Go, and carry stones back to the pasture. Yes, it will be hard work – some soft, young lads might say back breaking. But you are tougher than them. We will build a corral, and it will pay dividends. Once it is built, the sheep will be easier to herd, and our toil will be lessened."

The miserable old bastard, I thought. The sheep are not enough for him – now he wants to get obscene by tormenting and dominating a younger, stronger male than himself.

He wants to break me.

We will see who is broken in the end.

CHAPTER XXV

Chiron questioned the existence of the gods?

On the first day of my new project, the gods undoubtedly intervened by raising the temperature commensurate with Hades.

The heat made the quarry seem twice as far from the pasture as it really was. And the rocks twice as heavy.

I would lift a rock unto my shoulder and slowly tote it back to the pasture. In spite of my enormous strength, I teetered under the crushing load. The staggering walk back to the pasture seemed endless.

I dropped the first rock where Democulus indicated with a point of his staff, then reached for the goatskin of water. I was perspiring so profusely a small puddle pooled at my feet.

Before my hands reached the goatskin, Democulus brought his staff down hard, inches away from my fingers.

"Not yet, young buck. Not yet. If you take a swig of water every time you casually bring back a pebble from the quarry, there will be no water left before it gets hot. The sun is not nearly over head yet."

I felt a heat grow within me, far greater than that of the expanding sun. I had felt this heat before – when I broke the wolf's neck and again when I liberated Acis from his scalp. But this was different. The heat smoldered; I felt I could contain it until the proper time for it to erupt.

I felt a surge of resolve and energy as I returned to the quarry. I carried another stone then another, and another still. Had the gods given me strength, or was there a higher power contained within myself? I worked with a frenzy, and by sunset enough stones had been carried from the quarry to construct the corral.

I nearly collapsed beneath a tree from exhaustion. Then, Democulus approached.

"Do you think this impresses me, young buck? Why, when I was your age, I could work circles around you. You think you've worked hard today? Wait until tomorrow!"

Democulus had led the flock back to his lair earlier, and before he returned home for the night, I told him I would sleep in the woods this evening as it was hot, and I was tired.

"Make sure you're still here in the morning, young buck."

He began to walk away, then paused and turned to me. "You think I'm ill-tempered, Polyphemus? If you're not here at dawn and ready to work, I will be ill-tempered beyond imagination. And without you, my ill-temper will be unleashed on the sheep for whom you seem to feel compassion."

When he was gone, I arose and walked into the woods. My fatigue was gone. I had great energy and clarity of thought and purpose.

In little time I found what I sought – a long, thick limb that had fallen from a tree. I picked it up and felt it in my hands. It was dense and heavy.

I returned to the spot where I would later sleep, but first, before slumber, I drew my knife and began to carve and whittle. There it was beneath the stout limb I had retrieved. I could see it clearly beneath the knots and bark – it was merely a matter of cutting away the excess.

And soon, there it was in my hands. A staff; a magnificent staff – thicker than a man and longer than a cyclops.

CHAPTER XXVI

I awoke before dawn and waited for him. Then, as the sun rose, red and bulging, I saw him, driving the sheep to the pasture, bellowing at them and poking them with his staff. Then, he approached me.

"Well, well – you're still here, Polyphemus. In a way I'm disappointed. Now I have to supervise you, instead of giving my sheep their discipline lesson." He paused and smiled obscenely. "I love the sound they make when I discipline them – that squealing, bleating sound; very much like the sound a child makes when being raped."

With that he jabbed one of the sheep sharply with the staff. Then he jabbed another, even more viciously. And the sheep made the sound he had described. I looked at him. Beneath his loincloth there was a growing bulge.

"Tell me, Polyphemus. Did you have supper last night, or were you too worn out to eat? I thought so. You must be famished. You need a hearty breakfast before you begin your labors. Make yourself useful and start a fire."

I stood motionless and stared at him. I could almost hear the rush of my blood.

I knew that it would be soon.

"Don't dawdle, boy; I'm in a rare, magnanimous mood. I'm not offering you porridge for breakfast. You should be on your knees showing appreciation – I'm going to provide you with a feast fit for the gods – a feast of fresh mutton!"

I remained motionless, as still as a statue. Democulus was glaring at me, his eye dilated with hate.

"Fetch your knife and open the throats of three sheep – now! I'll do the drudgery of skinning and gutting them, proper host that I am."

I remained still. The sun above grew in size, a red angry globe. A bead of sweat formed on my brow and dribbled down my face.

"Oh, I see now," continued Democulus. "You haven't got the cock or the balls to slaughter a sheep. The young buck is ball-less! This may be the most magnanimous day of my life. I not only will share my tender mutton with you, but I'll share my cock with you as well."

He thrust his hand down his loincloth and began to stroke. His hand pumped, gaining speed. Finally, he stopped, fully erect. Then, he dropped his loincloth.

"Come over here, Polyphemus. Let me share my virility with you. Drop to your knees before me and open your mouth wide. Or is it a mouth? I don't think it is a mouth at all, but a large wet pussy below your nose."

I complied. I walked slowly and knelt down before him. He looked absurd with his loincloth tangled around his ankles.

I reached out toward his organ, then raised my hand to his stomach and shoved.

He toppled over and fell on his back. His curses frightened the sheep.

"You bastard – you punk, bastard! You'll regret that – I'll teach you!"

He arose on unsteady legs and grabbed his staff. He swung wildly, and I sidestepped his blows with little effort.

Then, again, I stood motionless and allowed him to pummel me at will. He looked ludicrous as he flailed, foam and spittle flying from his mouth. Did the malignant old bastard really think he was my match? His blows barely stung.

Finally, as he was nearly spent, I grabbed the staff from his hands. I looked at it with mock disdain, then snapped it in two as if it were a twig.

"Democulus, my friend, I think you need a bigger staff."

I grabbed the giant staff I had carved the night before from behind some brush.

"Yes – yes, this should do nicely!"

I struck him on the side of his head with my gift; he fell to the ground, stunned.

"A much bigger staff, Democulus."

I reached down and rolled him onto his stomach. His curses were punctuated by wheezing sounds.

I tore off the loincloth as he kicked and thrashed and parted his wrinkled buttocks. The small round opening was withered and covered with matted hair. Then, I held the straight end of the staff to the opening and shoved.

His scream brought panic to the sheep and curdled my blood.

I shoved again, and the staff disappeared by a third. Then, I lifted my employer by the staff handle and raised him over my head. Shock and a gurgle of blood stifled further screaming.

First by inches, then by feet, Democulus body slid down the thick shaft, until the end burst through his mouth. Horror was frozen in his open eye, his face grotesque and contorted. He was skewered from end to end.

I dug a hole at the site of the corral and planted the staff upright with the impaled corpse held firmly.

Then, I fashioned a plaque which I hung around my macabre sign post, which bore an inscription:

This flock is the property of the cyclops, Polyphemus.

CHAPTER XXVII

It appeared that my livelihood was indeed to be shepherding, now that I had inherited a flock from kindly Democulus. But recent events had been stressful, if indeed unnerving. I needed to talk to someone; someone with a sympathetic ear.

I found Chiron in the grove where we had usually met. He greeted me as I approached. It was as if he knew I was coming and was waiting for my arrival.

"Ah, Polyphemus – I missed you these past few days. Have you been ill? You look a bit tired and haggard."

I felt like falling to my knees before my friend and mentor, but then, recent memories made that position ill advised.

"I thank the gods – whether they exist or not – that you are here, Chiron. I need to talk with you."

"Yes, yes my boy, but first, sit beneath the shade tree. You look exhausted and unsteady on your feet."

"Chiron, I have done something – something that is of, well, questionable virtue."

Chiron looked down upon me with his infinitely compassionate eyes.

"Oh, my dear lad, what could you have possibly done? I've concluded that you have compassion and conscience – and, in all modesty, under my tutelage you are developing principles. But you are so hard on yourself! Tell me – tell what you have done to warrant your brow beating."

I looked up; oh those eyes; those loving, caring eyes.

"I have murdered Democulus."

His eyes changed.

"You did what?!"

"I murdered Democulus, Chiron. And not in the heat of passion.

It was carefully premeditated, although my passion drove my plan."

I looked at Chiron. There was incredulity in his expression – and something else.

"He was a foul, disgusting sadist; loathsome and vile in every way. I murdered him, Chiron, and in a horrible fashion. I impaled him on an enormous staff that I had fashioned for that sole purpose. And I mocked him as he died."

Chiron seemed flabbergasted.

"You – you murdered Democulus? You impaled him?"

"Yes," I replied, in a cracking, sheepish voice.

What happened next challenged my sense of reality.

Chiron reared up on his hind legs and began to pirouette like a crazed dervish. He spun and danced and whinnied with demonic glee.

"Chiron," I implored. "Chiron – please, stop. I've… I've never seen you like this before!"

He stopped, dizzy and exhausted, and walked up to me. Then he reared up again, in order to be tall enough to take my head and hold it lovingly to his breast.

"Oh my – oh my dear, dear boy. You killed Democulus. You did what neither I nor the gods had the gumption to do. You murdered him! And not in some vaguely humane way, but you impaled him like a worm on a hook.

Oh my dear boy – I've never felt so proud in my life!"

Then, he released my head and said ever so slyly,

"If per chance shepherding does not pan out, you have a brilliant future as a public servant."

CHAPTER XXVIII

As Chiron had taught me to always complete what I had started, I finished construction of the corral and assumed responsibility for the sheep.

Galatea, after her own whorish fashion, spoke wisdom.

They were my children. And we were good to each other.

I became their provider and protector, and they provided me with milk and wool, both of which I could use for myself and also use in trade and barter. I tended to them and they gave my life purpose. They were indeed, my children.

I had names for all of them, and, try as I may not to, I had my favorites.

I had found a large cave for our home, which came with an immense boulder that fit perfectly over the entrance. And thus it was. My days were spent shepherding, milking the ewes, making cheese and wine and, as time permitted, visiting Chiron in the grove. I still had much to learn, as he would happily remind me.

One morning, after I had returned my children home after grazing, I met with Chiron at our usual spot. I wanted to confer with him about my dreams.

"Chiron, of late I am visited in my sleep by dreams. I have always dreamt, but more often now than before. I feel my dreams have more portent and duplicity than in the past."

"Dreams can be wonderful, my boy. They can soothe our spirits and provide messages, often through symbols."

He paused. His expression became grave.

"Or, Polyphemus, dreams can turn into nightmares. "

"Sometimes, Chiron, my dreams seem more palpable than what I experience when I am awake. Sometimes I do not want to awaken."

"Do you want to die, Polyphemus? Do you want to enter the realm of spirit and shadow? Or, perhaps, there is no realm at all, but only void."

"I have dreams that have magic in them – and a sense of harmony with the dream world. And in some dreams, Chiron, there is love. If I were to die during one of these dreams of harmony and love, would I live on within the dream world, and depart from the world of strife and suffering?"

Chiron looked up, staring at the heavens. Were there answers etched within the shapes of the clouds?

"You ponder the way I once pondered, Polyphemus. You ask the same questions I asked, oh so long ago.

Were you to die during a dream, yes, I believe you would leave this world which is rife with grief and sorrow; a world of agony and loneliness. But with all of my years and all of my wisdom, I do not know if the world of dreams would claim you and you could live on in this superior realm. There are seers and philosophers who believe there are many worlds and dimensions parallel to our own, but I have not observed sufficient evidence to draw a conclusion."

Again, Chiron looked above. Perhaps the clouds did speak to him, or the stars, waiting for the sun's descent so they could glimmer signs on the night's dark canvas.

"I believe that all of us, Polyphemus, have power. Whether the Fates and gods exist or not, we at least to a degree can determine our own lot. If the world feels cold, you can build a fire. If the land is barren, you can plant and sow. And if love has been lost, that does not mean the search for love must end. And if the Fates and gods intervene and your goals are hindered, you can look within and persevere."

"You are wise, Chiron. In so many ways you are wise. When we met you told me you had the prophet's gift.

In one of my dreams a messenger told me of the great war in Troy. I heard of the wooden horse that brought triumph to the Greeks and gifted doom to the Trojans. I heard of a reluctant warrior king who devised the horse; inciting the wrath of gods who doomed him to years of wandering as he labored to return home.

And I heard of a tragic young woman, beautiful and cursed with the gift you have – the gift to see and know what has not yet happened. This young woman is Cassandra, and, once in a dream she saved me from drowning.

I must know more. Can you look beyond, Chiron, and tell me more of her?"

A tremble travelled down Chiron's face. Then, he smiled. It was a smile of sadness - of sympathy.

"Yes, my boy, I can tell you more than will ever be told by your dream messenger.

I will tell you of Cassandra."

CHAPTER XXIX

"Once, there was a little girl who was different from all of the others. Her name was Cassandra.

She was a beautiful little girl, with hair and eyes dark as night – but she was feared by her father, a mighty king.

Her father believed his sons should be strong, and his daughter silent.

But she could not be silent.

As far back as she could remember, Cassandra could look upon the world and see not just what was there, but what was to be.

Her father, Priam, King of Troy, ruled a mighty kingdom that was protected by impenetrable walls – walls as thick as the forest and as high as the mountains. And the kingdom within and beyond those walls was further protected by a brave and fierce army which loved their king and their kingdom.

Now, under the rulership of Priam, there was peace and prosperity, and the king believed he was a strong and wise ruler, and as long as he was king it would always be so.

But his daughter Cassandra could see beyond what her father believed and had visions of what was to be.

And because of this, the king hated his daughter.

CHAPTER XXX

Once, when she was only eight, Cassandra was playing along the seashore, holding strangely shaped seashells to her ear and listening to magical sounds.

The sounds were like the sea and like the wind. They were a whisper and a roar. And as she listened, the sounds became a voice.

As she listened to the voice from the seashell, a group of fishermen cast off from the shore.

There were twelve fishermen on a small skiff, setting off from the shore, but before they left land, she saw eight. The voice whispered in her ear and told her secrets of what was yet to come.

The sky grew black, and Cassandra felt a chill. Then came the storm.

She looked upon the fishermen, fading in and out of view between the growing waves.

She had often seen anger in her father's eyes – a frightening anger, when she would run to him and speak to him of what she had seen of things that had not yet happened.

And now she saw that same anger, welling in the sea itself.

The small boat was buffeted by the waves. The waves appeared to Cassandra as enraged warriors, shaking and fluid, growing in size and wrath.

The fishermen on the boat bounced amidst the assault. They were men of the sea, who lived off the sea's bounty. They knew no fear. It was the land that offered danger; the danger of wolves and other wild things. The danger of men.

The sea was their true home, and they would often provide offerings to their protector, Lord Poseidon. He would assure safe passage, regardless of the irrational wrath and tumult of the black water and merciless waves. Or so they believed.

But Cassandra knew better. She could see the brewing storms before Poseidon himself knew of them, and for this, she was hated.

CHAPTER XXXI

The sky dropped as the ocean rose. The sea was hungry, and its belly gurgled.

The fishermen looked upon the famished sea and the black, drooling sky, and they knew.

They knew that their belief in protection and safety was illusory. They knew that nothing and no one were safe, and that they felt betrayed. They knew that death brewed in the sea, and the gods were either helpless or indifferent.

The first wave crashed upon them, shredding their sail – but they held fast.

Then, the second wave struck, and the brave fishermen lost their grip.

They were sucked down into the foamy vortex. When they arose from the breathless depths, four of them were gone.

For Cassandra, it was a scene like so many before. A scene that played in repeat; an encore of death and tragedy. A scene where the shock and horror were diluted, because she had already borne witness to the brutal absurdity of the event in her mind's eye – the mind and eye of a prophetess.

As the little girl grew into young womanhood, so did her beauty grow, along with her gift of prophecy. Gift? Perhaps, if the future contained visions of peace and harmony; but alas, these were blotted from her vision. No – it was a curse – an affliction – for what she saw was darkness and destruction; she saw flames of evil immolating the good.

They thought she was mad. Priam's mad princess, whose black eyes shimmered with madness as she stared, trancelike, into the abyss.

She became a curiosity among the Trojans, and even when her prophecies came to fruition, she was never believed.

Some believe Cassandra was not cursed until she became a young woman; and that the curse was inflicted by Apollo himself. It was said that she rebuffed his advances, and as punishment he spat the curse into her mouth that she would never be believed.

The gods. So quick in their wrath – so slow in their mercy.

Once, when she was 12, and her young womanhood began to burgeon, she stared into a pond and saw the reflection of a young boy who was part beast, gazing up toward her, tears of yearning flowing from his one immense eye.

She reached into the pond, and for a moment felt the touch of his hand. She pulled, trying to bring him to the surface – then the reflection dissolved. She shuddered, clasping her hands over her eyes. She did not want to know the sadness of his life; the horror of his fate.

And the absurd cruelty of his destined lot.

But Cassandra knew.

CHAPTER XXXII

As she matured, she grew more isolated. Unlike her royal siblings, she had no entourage. Even her servants tried to tend to her needs in her absence.

Her fellow Trojans would look upon her and avert their eyes. She was despised and feared; the beautiful mad woman who was loved and then cursed by Apollo. Was it true? True or not, the common people chose to believe. And so it was, the daughter of the king an outcast among her own people.

But she was an outcast who demanded respect. She had stood up to a god, and she was, after all, the daughter of Priam and Queen Hecuba. And, was it not said, that the gods often spoke to those who were mad?

In her dreams, Cassandra would see many things and hear many voices. She felt so alone when awake, but sleep would take her into a different realm, sometimes inhabited by others like herself.

One night as she slept, Cassandra heard a woman's voice speaking to her. The voice was gentle, but powerful, and the words spoken were wise.

It was the voice of Athena.

"Cassandra," said the voice, "Cassandra, listen to me. I know you, and how you have suffered. You have been chosen. The bearer of truth is hated by both gods and men. But I, Athena, will do my best to provide you with succor and protection; but always remember – I am not Zeus – I am a woman as are you, my precious Cassandra."

One day, as she walked along the seashore, she shivered with premonition.

She tried not to see as she held her hands over her tightly closed eyes; but to no avail.

She saw the image of her brother, Paris. Charming, handsome, callow Paris – transfixed by what he saw.

He had seen the face of the most beautiful woman in the world and was driven mad by desire. He had seen the face that would launch a thousand ships. He had seen the face of Helen.

CHAPTER XXXIII

Cassandra knew that he must have her. There were stories she had heard, though they had never been spoken.

There was a story that there was a contest among the goddesses as to whom was the most beautiful.

Eris, the goddess of discord, had interrupted an important wedding held on Mount Olympus that was attended by all of the important deities.

She threw a golden apple inscribed with "for the fairest" into the throng of celebrating goddesses. Ah, the vanity of goddesses! Each believed the apple was intended for her.

In due course, the field was narrowed to three: Athena, Aphrodite and the wife of Zeus, Hera.

Zeus was asked to be judge, but he wisely demurred.

Zeus told the goddesses to seek out a handsome young

prince who was tending sheep on Mount Ida, near the mighty city of Troy. This young prince, it was said, had a keen eye for beauty, and it would be prudent that he be the judge.

This young prince was Paris.

He had been isolated by his father Priam because a soothsayer had warned that this handsomest of princes would someday be the ruin of Troy.

Cassandra knew this, but had she spoken the words, she would have been scorned and disbelieved.

The three goddesses appeared before Paris; he was dumbstruck in their presence. Then, they told him his task.

He was told not to judge the goddesses based on their beauty. No, the goddesses each offered a bribe, and he was to choose the bribe that appealed most to him.

Athena offered him glory – that someday he would lead Troy to victory over the Greeks and vanquish their lands.

Hera offered him power – that someday he would be lord of all the mortals in all of the world.

Aphrodite offered him what she knew he yearned for most – she offered him the most beautiful woman in the world.

And it was to Aphrodite to whom he awarded the apple.

CHAPTER XXXIV

And it came to pass. There came a day when Aphrodite lead Paris to the island of Sparta, where King Menelaus received him as an honored guest. Menelaus, who was wed to Helen.

Helen, of her own accord or by the bitch Fates, was as infatuated with Paris as he was with her. And one night, when Menelaus was visiting his brother Agamemnon, Paris spirited fair Helen off to Troy.

The die was cast.

All of the Greek kings and chieftains rallied around their dishonored brother in keeping with their oath of loyalty. They were primed for war. Not that they needed an excuse.

For generations all of the Greeks had been obscene with bloodlust for an opportunity to wage war upon Troy.

The taking of Helen and disgrace of Menelaus were received as a blessing from the gods.

But as Cassandra shut her eyes more tightly she envisioned another king; this one a dissenter. He appeared to be more a tiller of the soil rather than a warrior, as he pushed a plow through a field with his infant son playing in the background.

She knew him. She knew that his one desire was to stay home and love his wife and son and make things grow in the fecund soil of his kingdom.

Cassandra knew his name and saw him – and herself – engulfed by the flames of the heartless Fates.

And she screamed. And as she screamed in horror, she heard another scream, from a distant place – the scream of the beast boy, her kindred spirit, Polyphemus.

CHAPTER XXXV

"I must know more, Chiron. Tell me more of the gods and men of the tragic war. I feel connected to them, our destinies woven together by the bitch Fates." Chiron appeared weary. Weary with life; weary with knowledge. To know. To know more than one ought to know. Curses come in many guises. To see and to know too much is one of them.

"Take caution, Polyphemus. Learn what you can; know what you must. Take lesson in Cassandra's plight. The gods can wreak terrible vengeance – whether they exist or not."

"I'm willing to risk, Chiron. Tell me more of those who

played for the gods' amusement on the stage of Troy."

Chiron saw the determination of his friend and student. He lowered his head and sighed.

"I will not tell you, Polyphemus.

But you can listen and hear the tales of those who were players at Troy in their own words. Come."

Chiron led me to a small hollow within the grove. We stopped before an ancient oak. It was gnarled and twisted, with strange knots on its bark that resembled eyes.

"Sit beneath this oak, Polyphemus. Sit within its shade and be still. Listen to the silence and you will hear."

CHAPTER XXXVI
ATHENA

"In the eyes of the gods, the lives of men are like insects, seen from the celestial heights of Mount Olympus.

But we gods and goddesses are not immune to boredom, and for our amusement we often descend, and condescend, to the earthly sphere that separates us Olympians from the sulfurous bowels of Hades.

Often, we assume the guise of mortals, and mingle among them. Frequently they fall into our favor – or disfavor.

I never was a child. I sprang, mature, from the head of my father, Zeus.

I was his favorite child; his grey eyed goddess of wisdom and war.

When I looked at the insects below, I saw much war and little wisdom.

But there were some below moving about in the human hive who were different.

There was the tormented girl who piqued the gods' wrath with her prophecies.

The gods are more often than not, cruel, and insanely patriarchal. They made the tormented girl's lot one of constant misery – especially that bastard Apollo.

But I have no fear of the gods. My father rules over them all, and I wield his shield and thunderbolt.

I am a fierce goddess – the goddess of war and protection. And I have taken pity on the hapless, tormented girl; the girl who sees the web of the Fates before it has been spun.

The girl Cassandra.

CHAPTER XXXVII
ODYSSEUS

"Why do men make war? As if life, with or without intervention from the gods, is not horrific enough.

There are men who are born to wage war. Men who are intoxicated by the chaos and destruction of mortal combat; seduced by the flames of vanquished cities and the screams of the people who inhabit them.

These men hate life and worship death and are ingenious at concocting absurd rationales for amassing armies and crossing the seas to kill and subjugate another people.

These men do not love their families or their homelands. These men love one thing – imposing their will and getting obscene over the keening wail of the dying, who in death bleat and cry like slaughtered lambs.

I am not one of those men. I must never become one of those men.

But, what if one is compelled to join forces with legions that one despises? What if good men are conscripted to become allied with barbarians – or suffer dire consequences? Men have been shamed and murdered for not closing ranks with their countrymen, and for a king such as I, such a demur would be worse than abdication.

I love my island kingdom and I love more my wife Penelope and son Telemachus. If my land or family were attacked, I would defend them with absolute conviction and ferocity. But every day the drums of war are beaten more loudly by my fellow chieftains, deafening our kingdoms of reason. The poets have been co-opted by the warmongers and sing of the evil of the Trojans. The people, simple in their ways, are swayed with frightening ease. The poets sing of the glory of war, and of rewards from the Olympian gods for fighting bravely. The carnage and horror of battle are redacted from their verse.

I must be stalwart. I must resist. I have always been lauded for my wiles, and now, I must devise a plan by which I will not be a prostitute to war.

And if I fail? Then I must devise a plan to end the war as victor – and return to my home and family."

CHAPTER XXXVIII
AGAMEMNON

"For the great warrior king, war is not an option or a choice – war is destiny. The gods would disclaim this and proclaim that we mortals blame them for our own behavior.

But the gods secretly encourage men such as myself, for they understand the ruthless far more than they respect the merciful.

For countless generations, Troy tantalized us within an always uneasy state of peace. We of the house of Atreus are the most warmongering of a warmongering people, and Troy – wealthy, prosperous Troy, impenetrable behind its great walls – was simply too much to resist.

But façades are important. We Greeks have long been in

the vanguard of civilization. Our art, poetry and architecture – our laws and philosophy; our science and mathematics, all render the rest of the world barbaric by comparison.

So alas, wars of unprovoked aggression make cracks in the façade. We are, therefore, ever vigilant to keep our eyes wide open for excuses that have some semblance of credibility by which to unleash our great armies and launch our great ships.

The gods have blessed us with Helen."

CHAPTER XXXIX
HELEN

"I am the most beautiful and desirable woman in the world. Am I immodest? To say less would be disingenuous.

It has been said that my father is Zeus, but so many claim to be progeny of the gods. It does not matter to me. Being descended from the gods would be superfluous.

Men, with their strength and skill with arms, believe they are powerful. These men would drop their arms and surrender upon one brief glimpse of me. That is power.

Am I vain? Am I deluded in believing that I and I alone was the cause of the brutal war between the Greeks and the Trojans? When Paris took me back to Troy, the Greeks to a man pledged to go to war to bring me back to Menelaus.

Except for one. The King of Ithaca. He alone demurred. He must have been blind."

CHAPTER XL
PARIS

It was prophesied that I would be the ruin of Troy. But when I looked at Helen, I did not care.

My father Priam had expelled me from the city. I, a prince

of Troy, had been relegated to tending to the sheep in the fields. My father; he believed in the prophets – except for the prophecies of my sister, Cassandra.

Had he listened to her, Troy would have thrived forever, and the sea would be engulfing the countless corpses of Greeks, and their thousand ships.

But my father was proud and stupid. He had no more love for me that he had for Cassandra.

Why should a son who never wronged his father be loyal to him, when that son has been shunned and despised by him? How can a son love a father who stifles the paternal impulse in favor of the rants of disheveled vagabonds bearing their reptile oil elixirs and fabricated prophecies?

I close my eyes and envision another tormented being – one who tends to sheep as I do and has grown to love them as his children. Who is this brother of mine, hated by a father who is even more powerful than mine?

This brother, forced to turn a blind eye to the obscene lot cast upon him by insane gods and malignant fathers."

CHAPTER XLI
HECTOR

"Only one warrior in the world was my match in combat; the champion of the Greeks, Achilles. Long before the Greeks besieged us, he and I knew we would cross swords in mortal combat. We both knew that neither of us would survive the absurd contest – although he would avoid the pyre a bit longer than I.

He knew of his fate from his goddess mother Thetis, and I, from my sister Cassandra. I, of all the family, was immune to her curse, and when she whispered to me my fate, I knew. She could not look at me in the eye, shamed by what she knew.

I knew her gift. She and I were stitched upon the same tragic tapestry. Our lot was doom, whether the gods favored us or not.

There is a bond between brothers, and Paris was my younger brother. My feckless, beautiful baby brother.

I always watched out for him. I protected him, and he needed protection.

I was my father's favorite, and Paris was shunned. He had the physique of a warrior, but the soul of a shepherd. I would often watch him with the sheep he tended. He was gentle, loving and nurturing. I wondered if he knew the ultimate destiny of his charge, or if perhaps the concept and vision of spring slaughter had been wiped from his consciousness, possibly by one of the doting goddesses who also protected him; most likely Aphrodite. Paris had deemed her to be the fairest of all the goddesses. The vain and the superficial are ordained by the Fates to have affinity.

Today, I stood atop Troy's highest wall and looked out toward the vast blue sea. Soon, a thousand sails will appear over the horizon. The blue sea will become crimson.

Cassandra's breath is still warm upon my ear. I look down at the ground outside Troy's great gates. I see two warriors, exchanging blows in single combat. I am one of those warriors.

I am poised to deliver the deathblow, but my hand falters. My arm is tugged backward. It this deus ex machina – do the gods stay my hand?

Or perhaps my foe has just gotten the better of me."

XLII
THE FATES

I am Clotho, the spinner of the web of life. My sisters are Lachesis, who assigns the lots in life, and Atropos, who wields the shears that sever the threads connecting life to death.

We are blamed and vilified by the fragile race of men, but never praised or given offerings when fortune is good.

Even the Olympian gods have no power or influence over us. We are autonomous and without oversight. Yes, the gods intervene into the lots of men, but do they truly alter destiny? Perhaps it is the vanity of the gods to believe so – perhaps the gods are merely cogs in the machine we have devised and set in motion. We choose the manner in which men are both born and how they die.

How do we decide the lots of men? Is it random? Is it arbitrary – cruel for the sake of cruelty? Or beneficent for the sake of whimsy?

Or is it all fallacy?

What we weave may be illusion.

In truth, we Fates may not even exist at all."

CHAPTER XLIII

I smelled something unpleasant. Something earthy and pungent, as if from a stable, was poking at my nostrils.

It was Chiron's hoof, wiggling in my face.

"Wake up, my boy, wake up! The tree is tiring of your loitering."

I shook my head, breaking my reverie. It was as if I was emerging from a trance.

"And now, you have greater insight into the fall of Troy, Polyphemus. What have you learned?"

"I have learned much, Chiron. And I have learned nothing. The behavior and deeds of gods and heroes is no more noble and less venal than the deeds of the weakest and most common of us. Troy is a microcosm of the world; the tragic world in which I live and suffer with everyone else. The fall of

Troy is but one chapter in the fall of man."

Chiron looked at me. His eyes, moist and heavy with sadness.

"And the fall of cyclopses and centaurs as well, Polyphemus."

CHAPTER XLIV

The days became routine and uneventful. I honed my skills as a shepherd and grew to know my flock. Their behavior was markedly different since their liberation from Democulus (my, what a fine, mummified signpost he had become – proof that all creatures have redeeming values.)

I also continued seeing Chiron in the grove – Chiron, my mentor and best and only friend.

His patience with me was infinite (occasional equine outbursts not withstanding). There was so much that piqued my curiosity; so much more that he could teach me.

Archery was a lost cause, but Chiron taught me the use of the potter's wheel and the skills of the woodsman; and, although Sicily, the Land of the Cyclops, is blessed with rich natural flora, he taught me the craft of the farmer.

But he never strayed far from the esoteric. The big questions fascinated him; the questions for which even he could only suggest at answers.

"Now, pay attention, Polyphemus my boy. Today's lesson concerns cosmology."

I was already at a disadvantage, not knowing the meaning of the word. Fortunately, my ignorance was anticipated by my mentor.

"Cosmology, my boy, is the study of all that there is; everything, from the smallest of particles beneath our feet to the greatest stars beyond this tiny pebble of a world."

"The microcosm and the the macrocosm?" I queried.

"Yes, Polyphemus. Excellent. You are already familiar with the concept. If one can truly grasp the idea of the circularity of the finite and the infinite, then one can find perspective and context for all things."

"But Chiron—you seem to suggest that there is order in this world and beyond; but I have never seen order. I see only the god who has no face or form—the god Chaos."

I half-expected an exasperated whinny and a lump of turf kicked in my face, but Chiron held his composure.

"Some say we project order into the universe, while others maintain we project fragmented irrationality—what you characterize as chaos.

The universe is vast beyond comprehension, Polyphemus. We occupy a portion of this universe which is smaller than a drop in all the great seas. The scope and influence of the gods may very well be contained in that miniscule drop.

The gods. They speak to you in dreams. Have you ever wondered why these powerful gods seem to be so shy? When is the last time you actually saw one, Polyphemus?"

There he goes again, I thought. Chiron just could not conceal his skepticism of the existence of the gods. When he told me that neither he nor the gods had the courage to dispatch Democulus, was he expressing sarcasm?

Chiron—contemptuous doubter of the gods. He must be a true believer that they do not exist. Perhaps he is right. He has not yet been struck dead for his contempt.

Or, perhaps they feel no need to make haste.

There are those who tempt the Fates.

But what of those who tempt the gods?

CHAPTER XLV

By now, I had fashioned a home for myself and my wooly children.

I had discovered a large cave below the bluff with an expansive interior. It was large enough to accommodate my entire flock and me, with ample room for expansion. The stalagmite formations were varied in shape, and some actually were in the form of chairs and other furnishings, to which I plied the skills Chiron had taught me to shape and smoothen them for greater comfort. Ah, such a shame I rarely had guests.

And, for security, a large stone was near the cave's entry, which, with a little alteration from hammer and chisel, fit perfectly over the entry. The weight of the stone was immense, and I was confident only I had the brute strength to move it. How dare Chiron infer I was not the son of a god!

By my own admission, I am a son of a bitch.

CHAPTER XLVI

My children were thriving on the lush grass of my island's pastures, and the days began to blend with an anticipated calm. I had not seen Chiron for several days, and decided to meet him at the grove. Uncannily, he was always at the grove when I sought him, as if he knew beforehand that we would meet.

"Good morning, Polyphemus. Bright and early, as I'd hoped you would be."

He looked drawn and weary. I had never seen him like this. His demeanor spoke of fatigue and resignation.

"Polyphemus, have you ever wondered how I came upon your island? You surely realize this is not my native land."

"I have wondered, Chiron. I knew you were not born here. Frankly, I've never been sure where you call home. I thought, possibly, that you may have arrived here through some metaphysical means. I mean, before we met, I encountered Pan on this island, and I have no idea how he arrived here either. I . . . I suppose I thought that satyrs and centaurs are similar and can simply will themselves from one place to another."

Chiron let loose with a full-throttled, lip-fluttering whinny of disgust. I placed my arms over my face in anticipation of a salvo of turf.

"How dare you—how dare you compare centaurs with satyrs. Especially a centaur like myself with a lecherous drunken satyr like Pan."

He calmed down a bit and shook his head with sadness.

"Oh Polyphemus—where have I failed in my mentoring? This demands an emergency lesson. Now,
 pay attention."

I was rapt.

"Now, my boy, when contrasting two different phenomena, there are two basic means by which those phenomena differ. The first is difference by degree. Example: a large rock is different from a small rock by degree. Regardless of the size differential, both are none-the-less rocks.

Now, conversely, a rock is different from a man regardless of size; the rock and the man are essentially different.

Now, I postulate, my boy, that a satyr and a centaur are essentially different—and in many ways."

I knew what was coming. If only I could flee.

"Your task, my boy, is to explain those differences in minute detail."

At least he did not tip an hour glass with a wide funnel on end while reminding me that time was of the essence.

My mind reeled. The differences of degree were numerous, but the essential differences? I rolled the dice.

"A satyr walks upright—a centaur does not."

Chiron furrowed his brow. His lips fluttered, albeit with subtlety. One of his rear hooves scraped the ground.

"Look at me, Polyphemus. Do I crawl on my stomach, in reptilian fashion? Is my torso horizontal when I walk, or vertical? From waist to head I am straight and upright whenever I take a step. Try again."

My mind stretched. Pan and Chiron were the only satyr and centaur I had ever experienced personally. They seemed different in essence. This should not be so difficult.

"A centaur is wise and sober; a satyr is superficial and inebriated."

This time the lip fluttering was less subtle.

"The question is not are there specific differences between Pan and myself; the question is what are the differences between satyrs and centaurs in general. I can assure you that there are some satyrs who are tee totaling creatures of substance and there are some centaurs who suffer from chronic alcoholism and idiocy."

One final attempt before I incited a one-centaur stampede. Essential difference—I must think essential difference.

"A centaur is a man with certain aspects of a horse—a satyr is a goat with minor aspects of a man."

There; that should placate the egotistical old horse!

"Excellent—excellent my dear boy. We'll make a philosopher out of you yet!"

Before Chiron could utter another word, we both heard a nearby sound. It was a sound that, for me, was indelibly etched in memory.

It was the sound of music—flute music.

And then, stepping out from behind the trees, flute pressed to lips, stood Pan.

"Well, look who I have happened upon. If it isn't that old Clydesdale Chiron, with his stable boy, Polyphemus. Tell me, young cyclops, have you fed him his oats and brushed the fleas off his hide yet? We wouldn't want him to be hungry and uncomfortable now, would we?"

Chiron stepped closer to Pan and looked him up and down as if perusing a slightly anthropomorphized dung hill.

"Pan, what a pleasure to see you. To what do we owe this privilege? Did you need a break from fornicating with the squirrels?

"No," replied Pan. "I'm here to investigate the corrupting of a feeble-minded young cyclops by a lascivious old horse who fancies himself some kind of philosopher because he has an odd growth on top of his neck that gives him a vaguely human appearance. But, alas, Chiron, you can take the horse out of the stable, but you can't take the stable out of the horse." Then, with a sideways look of contempt, he addressed me.

"A satyr is a goat with minor aspects of a man. Indeed! And after introducing you to the pleasures of Dionysus—after allowing you to hear the sublimity of my flute music—and yes, after saving you from demonic bitches who would have torn off your gonads and played hot potato with them—this is the respect and gratitude you show me? Why, you're as hopeless as a centaur!"

The gauntlet had been thrown.

Chiron began to slowly circle Pan, all the while stomping his hooves and fluttering his lips threateningly. Then, he reared up on his hind legs and flailed at Pan, who deftly weaved and bobbed away from his opponent's blows as he tooted mockingly on his flute.

It was one of the most ludicrous sights I had ever beheld.

Chiron thrust a hoof at Pan—Pan ducked and parried, striking back with his flute in lieu of rapier.

A rhythm developed, a farcical dance of thrust and parry; two hooved oafs too clumsy to really do one another harm. I was hoping they would exhaust themselves before their hooves got tangled. Horses are often put down when they break a leg; but what of centaurs?

Then, Pan did something extraordinary.

Feigning to his left, he abruptly pivoted, catching Chiron off-guard. For a split second, all four of Chiron's legs were simultaneously on the ground.

Pan leapt high like an acrobatic frog and landed atop Chiron's back.

Chiron's expression was one of rage and astonishment. Reflexively, he began to buck in an attempt to shake his tenacious foe off his back—but to no avail. Pan's arms wrapped around Chiron's torso, and his legs were vice-like, shaking with strain as they clamped around his opponent's back and flanks.

And around and around they went, Chiron heroically trying to dislodge Pan from his back, and Pan determined to hold on.

The image they presented was by turns idiotically absurd and embarrassingly tragic. A sense of pathos was descending upon the scene. What was this doing to Chiron? A creature of immense bearing and gravitas? It must be devastating. For Pan, somehow, such buffoonery seemed appropriate.

It was time for me to intervene.

"That's enough, Pan. Get off his back. Now!"

Pan looked down at me from his spinning perch, his face twisted into a gleeful smirk.

"I'll get down when your erudite mentor surrenders. And if he doesn't surrender, I'll break his spirit, like I would any other uppity horse who doesn't know his place."

"Stop it right now. Get off. I mean it, Pan. Think of his dignity. This could destroy him. Get off now or I'll yank you off and bash your skull in against a tree."

"Keep out of this, Polyphemus. He can't hold on much longer. Just another moment or so and I'll buck him off, then you can savor the bliss of watching me shove his flute up his ass. And if he farts, it will be the finest music this fake flautist has ever made!"

I started moving toward them, to end the lunacy, when they both toppled onto the forest floor—toppled, without grace or ceremony, into a grotesque pile of legs, hooves, heads and horns jutting out from the asymmetrical heap.

Somewhere, at the bottom, there may even have been a flute—hopefully not lodged within someone's backside.

I observed them for a moment. Were they dead?

Then, I went into shock.

Both of them sprung up from the heap, laughing uncontrollably.

"Well, Professor Chiron, I do believe we got him."

"I must indeed agree, Doctor Pan. We had him going from beginning to end."

They continued to guffaw uproariously.

"Please—please Polyphemus . . ." Chiron could barely speak, he was so racked with laughter. "You've been so morose for so much of your life, we thought a mind-boggling prank like we just delivered would blow away the dark cloud that always seems to hover over you."

He was right. I was mind-boggled.

"We thought?" I was flabbergasted. "Do you mean to tell me you two know each other?"

Pan replied first.

"Yes, my muscular young cyclops. Chiron and I have known each other for years."

"Years, Pan? I think centuries is more accurate," replied Chiron.

"Well, if truth will have it, Chiron, we may be looking at eons."

"Please forgive us, Polyphemus." Chiron tried to sound contrite, but he could not suppress his chuckling as he spoke.

"We couldn't resist."

Pan found his flute and blew a couple of comical toots before speaking.

"You aspire to be the consummate shepherd—think of having the wool pulled over your eyes as an initiation rite!"

And with that, I joined in on the uncontrolled laughter.

Large goatskins of wine materialized as if from nowhere, only to disappear through the night by the combined magic of a centaur, satyr and cyclops.

CHAPTER XLVII

I awoke to the sound of flute music.

The sun seemed to be struggling over the horizon. Today, dawn would not come in a burst but in a reluctant flicker. The remnants of the night still darkened the forest.

I cleared my eyes and saw Pan.

He was sitting on the ground, cross-legged, playing his flute. The music was different. It sounded sad, almost dirge-like.

I looked about to locate Chiron, but he was nowhere to be seen. Pan stopped playing his flute and approached me.

"Chiron is not here, Polyphemus. He received a message from a raven while you were sleeping. There is trouble that he must attend to."

"Trouble, Pan? What kind of trouble? And where?"

Pan appeared distressed and reluctant to respond. Did he know more than he was willing to tell?

"Chiron has had many students through the years, Polyphemus. And he is fiercely loyal to them all.

As you know, he is exceptional among centaurs. Most of his kind are vile and vicious.

Chiron has received notice that one of his former students is in danger. A number of centaurs have been plotting to murder this former student. Chiron has departed in order to intervene."

I was stunned and fearful. Chiron, my gentle friend and teacher, rushing off in the dead of night to prevent his student's murder? His impulse was noble, but the mission seemed suicidal. My mentor was a far better teacher and philosopher than a warrior.

"In what direction did he go, Pan? I'll catch up to him. He can't do this alone."

Pan's eyes began to tear.

"He must do this alone, Polyphemus. He has known for years—longer than years—that this time would come. Whether ordained by the Fates or simply set in motion by random events in a dumb universe, this time was meant to be.

Chiron is my friend, Polyphemus, and I respect him as I do no other. But we are at loggerheads concerning the gods. I believe in them and pay them homage; Chiron mocks and disavows them."

"Where—where Pan! In what direction did he go? I must find him!"

No music from a magic flute could erase the sorrow etched on Pan's face.

"Go north. Follow the trails that take you north. Go, young cyclops—do what you must do, just as Chiron will do as he must do."

CHAPTER XLVIII

The island of Cyclops is not a small one, and my point of departure was near the southern shore.

How much of a head start had Chiron gotten? We cyclopses are deceptively fast, and our endurance is exceptional. But the flight of my dear mentor, I could only imagine, was at gallop speed (how annoyed he would be that I assumed he would traverse as a horse.)

The trails twisted and turned, and at points stopped altogether, only to begin again after the breaks. Where exactly was the destination? If only I had a map or some other means of orientation.

I kept going, zigzagging through the dense forest. I was drenched and breathless and would soon need to rest. Then, I heard sounds of struggle.

I bolted closer to the sounds and came to a clearing.

There, on the forest floor, I saw Chiron, cradled in the lap of an enormous muscular man.

"What have I done—what have I done!" sobbed the huge man.

I approached the two of them. Chiron was writhing in agony.

"You must be Polyphemus," the man queried. "Chiron has been asking for you. Praise Zeus that you have found us."

"Fuck Zeus, and all of his hoity-toity friends on Mount Olympus," Chiron growled through his anguish.

"Polyphemus, this overly muscled young man wearing the ostentatious lion's cloak is my former student—his name is Hercules, and, like you, he also failed archery."

Hercules looked up at me, his face awash with tears.

"Chiron learned that a group of vengeful centaurs led by his nemesis Nessus had set out to ambush me." Hercules lowered his head and kissed his friend on the forehead.

"I killed three of them with my bare hands, then others arrived and I began shooting at them with poisoned arrows."

Hercules began to sob and choked on his words.

"Then . . . then Chiron arrived. I had Nessus in my sights, but he moved suddenly—as if he had been aided by the gods—and my arrow found Chiron."

"Leave the gods out of this, Hercules." Blood began to pour from Chiron's mouth. "You didn't pay attention during archery class." He gagged as the blood pooled in his throat. "My own fault, I suppose. I should have kicked more turf in your face."

Chiron's face became fierce. "Go—go, Hercules. You can still catch up to them. Find them, and atone for your error. Make sure Nessus' demise is far less pleasant then mine."

Hercules held Chiron to his chest and wept softly.

"Chiron—I'm so sorry—plea . . ."

"Go! Go now while there is still time. Give me a moment with Polyphemus. I have something to say to him."

And, with a final caress on his mentor's head, Hercules was off, in pursuit of vengeance.

"Come close to me, Polyphemus." I knelt beside Chiron and cradled his head on my lap. There was great weariness in his eyes, but no fear. His breathing was labored, but his voice did not falter.

"Whether the Fates exist or not, Polyphemus, your lot has been a cruel one. But be strong and persevere.

Look at what you have done in your short life. You have been fierce and have wreaked havoc upon those who deserved violent ends. You are a protector as well as an avenger. Your shadow looms far and dark, making those who prey upon the weak and innocent shudder.

I have tried to be a good teacher to you, my boy, and I hope you have learned a thing or two from me. Keep learning. Stay brave and strong.

There are many things you could do, Polyphemus, but could any lamb be more fortunate than to have you as her shepherd? This is your calling. Cultivate other skills and nurture other passions; but you could be the greatest of all shepherds; as gentle as you are strong—predators beware."

Chiron emitted a long sigh. Blood spurted from his mouth but he was not yet finished.

"Take care, my son, and prevail."

And, with his last gasp. He smiled.

"Yes, Polyphemus. My son. Fuck Poseidon. Had I been your father my lesser half would have strutted like a proud stallion instead of a plodding Clydesdale. I love you, Polyphemus, my son."

And then he was gone.

I looked up into the heavens and roared in grief and rage. And then, I saw it.

I thought I knew all the stars in the heavens. On many nights I would stare endlessly above, marveling upon the small flickering gems in the sky.

But now, new stars shined bright.

Looming large in the southern sky, they flared rather than flickered. They spoke to me.

And as I stared longer, I knew.
Their shape formed the silhouette of a magnificent centaur.
Centaurus. Chiron would be with me forever.

BOOK II
ODYSSEUS AND DARKNESS

CHAPTER I

And so, my life as a shepherd resumed. Save for my flock—my children—I was alone in the world.

In the community of cyclopses, isolation is a defining characteristic. We intuit fair and reasonable boundaries, and disputes are a rarity. Seldom do we communicate.

I have developed an appreciation for fine wine. Grapes grow in abundance on my island, without cultivation. The soil is dark and rich. But I want the very best grapes for my wine, and so I have learned to grow the finest of all grapes. The corral which once contained the sheep has evolved into an arbor for the small vineyard I have established. Democulus remains on his pole, but the elements are as ill-humored as he was, and his dried, withered remains are easily buffeted in the breeze. I have placed a hat on his head and he now makes an exceptional scarecrow, keeping the pecking birds away from the grapes. I do believe he would approve.

CHAPTER II

It began as a day like so many others.

Sunrise—how do the poets describe it—rosy-fingered dawn? Today the poets are wise, and the day began with a sense of promise and rebirth.

I awaken just after sunrise. I awaken to the sound of my children. They need to meet the rising sun outside our cave— our home. They need to graze in the freshness of open air; to move about with freedom; to experience life without the restraints of paternalism that, in spite of all good intentions, can be oppressive and stunting.

But first, there is the stone at the entrance to my cave. Neither man, nor beast, nor cyclops can enter or exit my domicile with the massive stone in place. But only a cyclops— an exceptionally strong one such as I—can move the immense object that blocks the sun and silences the night. The stone gives me peace and security. My children are completely vulnerable to the wolves and predators of the world. They are safe with me behind the stone.

But I worry. To be honest, I am not sure myself how old I am. Of late, there have been times during the daylight hours when I have left the cave to harvest grapes or draw water and I have forgotten to roll back the stone and my children have been left vulnerable. I must be more mindful. I must be forever vigilant. I have no reason to believe that the gods and Fates have not made me their chosen one—their unfavored child. The one for whom suffering and calamity lie in wait— always ready for the opportunity of the forgotten rock.

CHAPTER III

I was tired. It was an ambitious day.

I herded my sheep to a pasture which was farther than

most, but the grass was greener and lush; thick and succulent, as if infused by the gods themselves with ambrosia and nectar. My children ate as if they never before had experienced sustenance.

As they feasted, I remembered I needed kindling wood. I ventured off into the woods, where I lost sight of my elder children—what harm? I was not gone long. And besides, the lambs, my precious infants, were protected within the impervious haven of my cave. Or so I thought.

A strange chill ran down my spine. Had I been careless earlier? The stone—had I rolled the stone over the cave entrance? My baby lambs were sleeping when I departed with their older siblings. Had I left them sealed and safe—or did I suffer a lapse, leaving them in a state of total vulnerability?

The moment I saw the clouds, I knew there would be tragedy. I knew things would never be as they once were.

CHAPTER IV

With kindling and huge bunches of grapes on my shoulders, I trudged back to my cave, my older children in tow. With every step, my heart raced faster, and my sense of dread loomed larger.

There was death and doom in the air. I looked about as we came closer to the cave. The birds who normally sang at this time of day were silent. The butterflies who once danced among the trees were in hiding. I began to tremble.

I arrived home. The entrance to the cave was wide open.

I wanted to avert my eyes, but I could not. It was strange. How many times had I exited and entered my home through that cavernous opening? Thousands of times? But I had never noticed the details and nuances of the opening—until now. It looked, as I grew nearer, like a gaping mouth, stretched to obscene extreme. Only the absence of Cerberus, the rabid three-headed dog who guards the gates of the underworld, made the entrance different from that of Hades. There should have been a sign above the portal, exhorting that those who entered should abandon all hope.

I was at the entrance. There were footprints in the soft, sandy ground—footprints of men. And there was an odor—one I had known before.

I shook with horror as I inhaled the stench of death.

CHAPTER V

The Greeks are a fascinatingly complex race. They have led the world of men in culture, philosophy, science—and militarism.

How can a race of people explore the big questions regarding truth, beauty, justice and idealism wreak so much suffering and carnage in their pursuit of power and empire? Surely they, of all people, would have devised a civilized method of conquest—a way to subjugate and co-opt other nations through reason and benevolence. But they are as brutal as they are intelligent.

Is such an extreme dichotomy the product of a random universe, or another cruel and ironic joke from the capricious and whimsical gods?

A soothsayer from a faraway place once told me there would be a monster in the far distant future—a man from the northern climes; a man who was an artist and a charismatic visionary, who had the gift to mesmerize and mobilize the masses—for the purpose of genocide and world domination.

Is life driven by absurd contradictions? Can the most vicious and vile among us also be capable of kindness and generosity?

Can the greatest of all sins be committed by the most radiant saints?

I inhaled again before I ventured inside. There was another odor along with the death stench that repulsed me instinctively.

I smelled Greeks.

CHAPTER VI

My children would ordinarily greet me with joy and excitement upon my return—but this time there was silence.

A small group of them, yearlings and weanlings, were cowering in a corner. Their breath was labored and they trembled, eyes wide with horror.

In another corner lay the carnage. Within the pile of mangled bones and fleeces; amidst the severed mass of entrails, I recognized the remains of my children.

There was Chloe—my sweet Chloe who would cuddle to my breast and purr as I stroked her back; and Phoebe, my playful Phoebe, who would delight in our game of chase, and squeal with joy when I caught up with her. And I could recognize in the twisted heap the mutilated form of Bolt, my strong and loyal little boy who would have grown to be a mighty ram. I know he put up a valiant fight.

There they lay—pieces of sinew dangling from their broken skeletons. Their eyes, so familiar to me, stared wide, frozen in shock and dread.

The Fates—malignant bitches every one, see only cruelty and devastation in the casting of their lots, and are blind to mercy.

And then I saw him.

CHAPTER VII

He stepped out in front of the others, out from the

shadows. There were twelve in all, plus their leader. I knew exactly who he was. The soothsayers knew of what they had spoken. Before me stood my mortal enemy—my gift from the Fates.

There was an offensive tilt to his posture—his body language. I looked at his face. He was handsome, but weathered from his travels.

The gods have indeed compensated the one-eyed cyclops with singularity of vision. I can stare at and through what I observe. And, as I stared at the man before me, I could see through his veneer. He raised his palms in the universal sign of peace and his expression displayed a placating humility. But I could see through it all. The arrogance, the swag and the smirk simmered beneath the thin membrane of deception. I knew he looked upon me as an ignorant brute, his natural inferior. Then he spoke.

"Sir, we are men from the land of Ithaca, trying to return home after our long war with Troy. But the gods have deemed that our return not be an easy one, and time and again we have been driven off course by storm and misfortune.

My men were starving, kind sir, and we beseech you to bear us no malice for slaughtering a few of your sheep in order to survive. I see that your flock is huge, and I pray that you would not begrudge our taking of a few."

Why do men aspire to exceed the cruelty of the gods? Since the dawn of time, men have been the recipients of the capricious and insane whims of the denizens of Olympus. One would hope this would inspire compassion when men find themselves in a state of power over their own kind, and especially so over the lesser creatures. But look at them—look at what men do. They feel a compulsion to one up the gods themselves.

I looked down upon him and his men. Their mouths were red with blood and their bellies were bloated with the flesh of my children.

The stone blocking the entry to my cave—my lair—my home is as easy for me to move as drawing a silk curtain across a window. For my Grecian guests, my violators from Ithaca, it is immovable and so heavy it would break the back of Atlas.

I was numb with horror. Slowly, I walked back to the entry and moved the great stone, blocking all exit. Then I returned to my guest, and spoke.

"Why did you not sate your appetite with the abundant grapes from my vineyard which are piled high? Look upon the cavernous baskets of milk and the mountainous cheeses before you. Clearly you can see the loaves of bread, only a day old, stacked like bricks against the wall. There is enough food to glut an army. Why? Why have you entered my home, without invitation, and committed such atrocities? You could have eaten yourselves fat, without murdering and devouring my children."

I thought I had spoken softly, but to the Greeks it was a roar, and they drew back by reflex.

I looked upon my savaged children. Were they truly taken from me forever?

As the tears welled in my eye, I knew I must be strong.

As I looked at the face before me, the arrogance and contempt, hidden beneath the facade of humility, disappeared. Now, I saw fear.

I looked at the lot of them, and suddenly, all sense of grief and heartbreak were quieted.

At what point does sanity take flight and madness fills the void?

I looked upon them and smiled gently. I raised my palms

upward as I had seen him do. A collective gasp of relief filled the cavern, and slowly, they approached me.

My demeanor became calm and solicitous. "My name is Polyphemus, and I understand. You were starving, and starving men hunger for meat. Is that not true?"

"Oh yes, yes Polyphemus," spoke their leader. "We meant no harm or disrespect. We simply behaved like starving men—we saw meat and we took it."

My smile broadened. Had I ever smiled so broadly before? My face felt as if it would crack.

"Indeed yes," I addressed the king of Ithaca. "A hunger for meat."

I looked down upon them. Their dread was dissipating. Surely if I intended retribution I would have killed them by now.

An excitement, irrational and exhilarating, was building up within me.

"Tell me, brave king of Ithaca, what is it like to eat meat? All of my life I have subsisted on the milk and cheese provided by my flock, and the grapes and other fruits which grow naturally on my island, as do the many grains from which comes bread. But meat? I have never tasted meat."

I was becoming jovial in mood. Perhaps these Greeks were not all bad. I would soon find out.

"I'm beginning to be intrigued by the idea of eating meat." I gave my audience a sly, one-eyed wink and followed with, "Growing up on a meatless diet doesn't seem to have stunted my growth, however."

The Greeks began to laugh uproariously at my quip. My humor seemed to them to be a signal of forgiveness. Why, taking away from me my last reason for living was merely an impulse driven by hunger—an unfortunate, tragic mistake.

I placed my hands upon my stomach, and a crude growl erupted from my innards. The sound put a chill on the convivial mood.

"I must admit I am in the throes of a conversion experience."

I stared directly into his eyes. Could he guess, this wily king of Ithaca—this schemer of destruction—this Odysseus?

"Why, it's past my suppertime, and I too have a hunger— for meat!"

I moved so fast they could not suspend disbelief.

I grabbed two Greeks, one in each hand. They tried to scream, but their vocal chords froze with fear. Twisting them upside down, I raised them above my head, then thrust downward, crushing their skulls. Their brains bubbled on the floor, a greyish pink pudding awash in blood.

Then, stripping their mangled corpses naked, I ate them both, devouring their meat, organs, bones, bowels and gristle.

"Waste not, want not," I declared to my remaining guests.

They were beyond panic. Two of them had defecated on the floor, as others were vomiting. All had receded to the farthest corner of the cave. Their brave leader stared, his face a mask of horror and incredulity. I stared back. I stared at him and through him. My vision pierced the soul of this sacker of Troy—this creator of deceit in the guise of a horse; the architect of death encased in wooden artifice.

And then I looked downward, below his groin, as the golden fluid of his piss trickled down his legs.

CHAPTER VIII

Odysseus is not entirely a stranger to me. Cassandra has spoken to me in dreams. Through her, I was introduced to the King of Ithaca.

Through Cassandra, I have seen his arrogant smirk as he and his chosen elite sprung the trap and descended from the bowels of the gift horse. Had there ever been a gift of such treachery? The horse. A gesture of honor and concession to the Trojans for their heroic perseverance? No. It was a monument to a man who would commit any deceit and dishonor to attain his ends.

The Greeks had no concept of honor.

Hector, Prince of Troy, confronted Achilles honorably on the field of battle. Upon victory, Achilles, the greatest of the Greek warriors, desecrated the corpse of his fallen foe, dragging Hector's body, bound to his chariot, around the walls of Troy.

Hector's mother was driven mad with grief. His father, King Priam, was broken. He was forced to meet clandestinely with Achilles, to beg for the body of his noblest son for proper departure to the gods upon the funeral pyre.

And now, Odysseus, champion of deceit, cowered before me, his feet immersed in a yellow puddle.

What schemes were fermenting in this brave king's mind as he gawked up at me?

Perhaps I should eat him now. No—I am not finished with him yet.

CHAPTER IX

It has been said that every man—and cyclops—has a fatal flaw; a weakness—a vice that leads toward the path to destruction. Like wine, for example.

Early in my life, I discovered that the preternaturally lush grapes that grow on my island, without the assistance of gods, man or cyclops, were a source of great pleasure and solace to me. Was I taught, or did I know by instinct that these grapes could be converted into wine? And when I became a grape grower, I learned the craft of making wine which was all the more potent.

Wine. Wine can make an ordinary woman look like a goddess. It can make great wounds seem like scratches. And, in excess, it can make serpents bent on your destruction seem like devoted friends, or like strangers driven by good will and circumstance.

CHAPTER X

After my delightful visit with my guests and having finished my excellent meal (I must admit, I may have overeaten, but Greek, flavored with contempt and arrogance, is quite excellent) I felt a drowsy need for sleep.

I imbibed a large flagon of wine, and prepared for bed.

As my eyelids grew ponderous, I looked upon the King of Ithaca. He seemed focused on the effects of my post-meal nightcap. What might he be thinking? His noble face became ferret-like as I drifted into slumber. I looked at the stone at the cave's exit. What if he and his fellow ferrets were to slay me as I slept? They had no way out. It would be more a suicide pact then a murder.

I slept soundly, after the gurgling in my gut settled down. I could not help but to wax poetic at the gastric rumble.

Ode to a Grecian Churn.

CHAPTER XI

I awoke at dawn to the baaing of my children. My houseguests were cowering in a corner.

It was time to herd my flock outside for grazing. And to place what was left of my murdered babies upon the funeral pyre. Placing a large blanket upon the floor, I put their remains in the center with gentle reverence and stoicism. Stoicism—ha! A philosophy invented by some other Greek bastard. And yet, I can see its purpose.

I placed my bundle over my shoulder, and, with a watchful eye on my guests, rolled the stone away and led the flock outside. The air was fresh and pure. I left the cave open for a few moments to release the death stench, then pushed it back in place when I exited.

Oh what chatter there must be now that I was out of earshot! The blend of dread and hate tumbling from those Greek lips must sound like—like bleating! Oh, the delicious irony. How could I not smile?

These vile interlopers have killed my only connection to what was good in my life—fatherhood, caring and love for other sentient creatures.

I know the madness has fully taken hold. What is left for me? If not for vengeance, there would be no reason to go on.

Ah, pity the poor Greeks.

CHAPTER XII

My flock has fed on the rich offerings of our always abundant pastures, and is ready to head home. Home? Greeks, like pernicious rodents, have infested our home. Rodents, contained and cornered, can be eradicated. But before the pests are exterminated, it would be only fair that I engage their leader in rational discourse—or at least discourse.

CHAPTER XIII

I move the stone aside, and immediately see ten pairs of eyes squinting from the sudden assault of sunlight. Is my math faulty? Ah, yes. The King of Ithaca arrived unceremoniously with twelve stalwart brethren. Two of them are gurgling in my intestines, leaving eleven pairs, including their leader. A far luckier number than the original thirteen.

My experience, alas, is that there are no lucky numbers.

CHAPTER XIV

I must give him credit. He stepped right up as I entered. Both fearful and defiant, he approached me directly, straining his neck to look up and face me eyes to eye.

"Polyphemus, lord of your land, Sicily, I beseech you. We are proud men—and I, as our leader, may be proudest of all. But I will gladly swallow my pride, and fall to my knees, and do something I never imagined I would be capable to doing. I will beg you on my knees, with absolute respect, for mercy."

You disgusting little shit, I thought. Kissing my ass with disingenuous flattery. "Lord of Sicily?" "Absolute respect?" I know who and what you are. How much mercy did you show the screaming Trojan children as you wrenched them away from their pleading mothers, and bashed the skulls of their sons and enslaved their daughters for whoredom?

I smiled solicitously, and cleared my throat. What is it about Greeks that desperately cling to the tonsils before descending down the esophagus, en route to the stomach? They are tenacious, even after being masticated and swallowed.

"Tell me, oh King of Ithaca. To you, the creatures you and your comrades slaughtered were a delicacy, a special treat on hooves. You murdered them not because you had to, but because you could. To me, they were my children—warm, breathing creatures who gave me love and received love from me. They were my only connection to love, and to what is good in life. Tell me—when you chased and subdued them— when you overpowered them and held them still before you slit their throats—when you heard their high-pitched, glass-shattering squeals—did you have an erection?"

For a long moment he stared, gaping, nonplussed. I waited a reasonable amount of time, then grabbed two of his comrades. They knew their fate, and squealed like pigs about to become pork chops.

I inverted them, their limbs flailing with a near comic desperation, and raised them above my head, to be crushed as they had witnessed their brethren crushed.

Then, I stayed my hand, and gently lowered them to their feet.

I signed, and sat upon a stone that I long ago carved into my favorite chair. Then, as one of the Greeks I had spared tried to wriggle away—like a dog crawling with his butt flush against the floor to relieve the itch of fleas—I reached for him and sat him upon my lap.

I was feeling paternal. Given my own relationship with my father, this did not bode well for the Greek.

CHAPTER XV

Gently, very gently, I stroked his hair and smiled at him. A benevolent smile, without threat or sternness; the smile of a wonderful father—a father who provides love without consequence or condition.

He trembled, eyes wide with astonishment, expecting a repetition of recent history—that I would bash his skull into pulp, without compunction or ceremony.

But, with a softening heart, I took his tiny hands in mine and squeezed, ever so slightly; a velvety compression connecting a powerful being to someone of childlike vulnerability.

"Can you feel my touch, little one, as I hold your hands in mine?" I queried. My eye sparkled with beneficence.

He looked about frantically, eyes settling on his leader for a clue—a direction to provide the answer that would please me, and, if not spare his life, perhaps prolong it. But his leader's face was blank and his eyes vacant.

I bounced him a few times on my lap, as would a playful father bonding with his toddler. But alas, as gently as I tried, the bounces rattled his teeth and bones, and exacerbated his terror. How could I calm his frayed nerves. Ah—perhaps with a tale!

"Let me tell you a story, little one. A soothing bedtime story."

He looked upon me with astonishment. Did he sense his fate? A difficult question, as I myself had not decided his fate, and the Fates themselves were fickle and arbitrary, bound neither by rules nor predictability.

"Once upon a time, there were two young boys.

One was beautiful and beloved by his parents. The other was a horrible brute, deformed with one huge eye in the center of his head, shunned by his beautiful mother, hated by his powerful father—a god with infanticidal impulses.

The omnipotent trinity of gods—the fearsome triumvirate of cosmic deities: Zeus; Hades and Poseidon—they reigned supreme.

The brutish boy was the son of Poseidon, the god of the seas.

Mighty Poseidon had his choice of women, be they mortal, goddess or nymph. He never coupled with a woman whose beauty would not blind the sun. If his unions were to result in the birth of a son, that son would, as a matter of course, be blindingly beautiful. If not, the male offspring would be accursed, a blight upon his father's stature. Such a son should be stifled; snuffed and silenced before his squalls offended

ˌboth gods and mortals alike.

And the other boy? Oh, what pride and joy he afforded his parents! His mother, Anticleia, beautiful but without pedigree, worshipped him at birth as if he were a small, golden-haired god.

His official father, Laertes, was a steady and decent man; an unlikely paternal progenitor. Rumors were persistent that the golden boy's true father was Sisyphus, betrayer of Zeus. Gods do not take kindly to betrayal, and in our cruel world the sins of the father are visited upon the son."

I was beginning to enjoy my role as story-telling father figure. I was experiencing new sensations. I felt giving, magnanimous; I was doting and avuncular, and compelled to tell a story that was both fascinating and comforting to my little guest. But why did he squirm so upon my lap? Perhaps my grasp on his shoulders was not firm enough, and he feared he might slip from his comfortable perch and take a terrible fall onto the cold, stone floor below.

I tightened my grip, and his screams echoed off the cavern walls.

"Oh goodness," I exclaimed. "Forgive me—sometimes I think I don't know my own strength!"

I lightened my grip—just a bit—and continued my tale.

"Now the golden boy and the brute never met as children, but the Fates had ordained that their paths would cross as adults. Perhaps they would meet on a beautiful springtime meadow, and both would be shaken by a shock of recognition. Then, somehow, they would intuitively know that their destinies were inextricably linked, and they would cast off their differences and embrace as brothers. And perhaps not.

Do the male deities, within their strutting patriarchy, believe they alone determine the course of events for humanity and other thinking creatures?

Well, let me tell you about the Fates.

They are the true mothers of good and evil; good fortune and misfortune. Clotho, Lachesis and Antropos. The spinners of our direction; the weavers of the frail thread that connects birth with death, and all things in between.

Oh, what bitches these Fates can be!"

I patted my little friend affectionately on his head, trying not to rattle his brains, and continued with my bedtime story.

"For you see, the Fates demand their amusement—and it struck them as amusing that the golden boy and the brute would hate one another with a molten passion—long before their actual paths crossed. The hatred was like a seed, imbedded in their unconscious, sprouting within the dark nooks of their psyches—nurtured by the steady hands of the Fates. And both lads, the brute and the golden boy, knew by instinct that the other was out there, somewhere in the world, and only time, ephemeral time, separated them."

I paused to ruminate. My, what a wordsmith I had become! Chiron must be lighting up the sky with beams of pride!

The young Greek teetering on my lap had assumed a glassy-eyed look, as if in a state of catatonic shock. He appeared so young, perhaps the youngest of all my guests, and the most innocent. For a moment, my own identity escaped me. Who and what was I? Was the individual of a few days ago dead, to be resurrected into what I am now?

Was I confident in my own intentions? Did I even have intentions now, or had I become a slave to impulse?

Were all of the Greeks imprisoned in my lair of equal guilt and culpability?

A soft sound rolled from my young guest's lips. Was it a sigh? A subdued cry for mercy? A feeble plea for the end to the madness?

Where had I heard this sound before? It had a baaing quality, not altogether human.

There was a similarity to the sound he made to that of my own children—my sweet innocent lambs.

With a deep breath I continued. I had begun a bedtime tale for the now shuddering lad, who I had unconsciously been bouncing on my knee, and I had a responsibility as both host and storyteller to provide a proper ending.

The sad boy jostling up and down looked exhausted and ready for bed. I must think quickly for the tale's resolution, lest I appear as an improper host.

"And then, one day, it happened. The two met, as full-grown males, eyes to eye. And both of them knew, without introduction, who the other one was. And both of them knew that neither would ever be the same again."

I smiled and looked deeply into the lad's eyes. Why did he look back with horror? Oh dear me, where may I have gone wrong?

Of course—the story needed a fairytale ending.

"And they lived tormentedly ever after!"

As the final words tumbled off my palette, I heard a profound growling from my stomach. When had I last eaten? Hunger can cloud and influence one's judgement. It can make reasonable men abandon reason and reach out with blind compulsion for food. Why, just look at my guests and their own tragic predicament.

I deftly lifted my little friend from my lap and placed him on the floor. How adorable he was as he scampered off to the cave's farthest corner. Why, he looked just like a puppy, wiggling away on all fours.

In the blink of an eye, I grabbed one of his brethren—a

fortuitously plump lad who coincidentally had been dozing during the recitation of my wonderful story.

He awakened and flailed in my grasp, his widened eyes enveloping his face. He needed to be taught a little lesson for sleeping during class.

I squeezed his head between my palms to draw his attention.

His brains exploded like puss from a compressed carbuncle. Oops. I was a bit over-zealous. Ah well—spare the rod, spoil the child!

What redundant fellows these Greeks be. Once again, with near perfect synchronicity, there was collective screaming accompanied by nausea and the soiling of loin cloths.

Am I losing count? I believe the mighty thirteen has dwindled to ten. And where is their stalwart leader, co-star of my wonderful story? I cannot see him—but then, there are many shadows in my cave.

CHAPTER XVI

I began to eat my supper with a sense of relaxed leisure.

And, why not? Who among the diminishing band of intruders would have the temerity—the backbone—to stop me? Was I becoming over-confident? I looked upon the survivors, hunched and cowering and dismissed my own question.

Now, I could fully savor my meal. Ah, the marbled meat of plump Greek rivals the ambrosia of the gods!

I was nearly finished, save for the delicious sucking of the marrow from the bones. What vulgar sounds I must be making as I sucked and slurped. I hope I am not being an ill-mannered boor. What would my guests think of me? But I cannot resist. I have been told that marrow contains a cornucopia of nutrients, and strengthens the immune system. Such an exceptional treat. Most things which are so good for us are not nearly so tasty. But most things are not Grecian, and nothing is more delicious than revenge.

CHAPTER XVII

There are some who savor wine prior to an excellent meal. Good wine can whet the appetite and heighten the senses—or dull them, if appropriate.

It can also make one amenable to conversing with others who otherwise would be deemed unfit for conversation.

I have always preferred my wine after my meal, as a fluid bridge between appetite and sleep.

After a hearty belch, I reached for my flagon of wine—the rich, heady wine for which we cyclopses are famous.

And then, he stepped out from the shadows and spoke.

CHAPTER XVIII

"Cyclops, I have beseeched you to temper your rage with an understanding of the predicament in which my men and I find ourselves. You have answered my pleas with wicked cruelty. We have begged for the stranger's due, which is known and respected by all of the kings of all of the lands in the world protected by Earth the mother and Zeus the father. But to all of this—all of the laws and all of the desires of the gods—you have been blind. And so—as a final entreaty, I offer you a gift. A gift of wine. But of no ordinary wine.

I offer you a gift of wine of such grandeur that even the gods covet the smallest of sips. This is wine like no other, fermented by Apollo's favorite priest."

I looked down on him, knowing that deceit and duplicity were the essential components of his nature. And yet—was my exuberant leap into vengeance leading me down the path of self-destruction? Was I to become another casualty of the sin of hubris?

"Tell me, Greek," I replied. "Do you think that having only one eye equates to only half a brain?"

I could see the cogs grinding with urgency inside his head. How would he answer? With strength and defiance? Would he throw caution to the wind and respond with the truth, bolstered by the hatred in his heart? Or, would he measure and calculate before responding, placing benefit and risk on the precarious balancing board that could tilt toward salvation, or destruction?

I could see through his façade, through his inherent duplicity. Part of him was focused on me, and part of him was focused on the construction of another wooden horse. He could not help being duplicitous—it was his nature.

He answered as a small shudder rippled through his brow and lips.

"Cyclops—please; your name sir."

Had I not already provided my name? If not, I would reintroduce myself.

"I am Polyphemus."

He actually bowed before me, in an embarrassingly disingenuous act of supplication. But I could see—I could see it all. He yearned to kill me; the more unpleasantly, the better.

"Lord Polyphemus—I believe that the eye is a reflection of the mind. One very large eye equates to a mind which is immense and powerful."

Lord Polyphemus? The ass-kissing little bastard. What to do with him? I could do many things—extreme things— without reflection or guilt. Should I grab him now and slowly wrench his limbs from his torso, listening to his screams as one would listen to an aria from a doomed Calliope? Or perhaps fill my largest cauldron with water and heat it to boil, and toss him inside for a bubbling demise?

Poached Greek, prepared properly with the appropriate spices, might be excellent.

No. He and I both deserve better.

CHAPTER XIX

"Who are you, my Greek guest?" I could be as disingenuous as he—as if I did not know who he was. I have always known.

"Tell me about yourself. Tell me—I'm curious.

Which of my children were murdered by your hand? Perhaps none. You have a superior and imperious demeanor. Perhaps you delegated their slaughter, not wanting to stain your patrician hands with the blood of the innocent."

He stood silent, digesting my words as I digested his comrade. His eyes darted up and to the sides, so fast it was almost imperceptible. He was measuring—assessing the parameter of the situation. He tried to conceal his hatred, welling up from inside, but I could see. Hatred, so molten it could ooze from his pores. His face, for an instant, grew crimson.

And then, the seething hatred abated. He took a deep breath, and spoke.

"I was born a prince, oh cyclops, but I grew up as a farmer, for on my small island of Ithaca, the prince and the common farmer toil side by side; we must in order to survive. And, as I toiled with my countrymen, my back grew strong and my hands grew large and powerful; and, at the age of twelve, I could wield a sword most grown men could barely lift.

When I was sixteen, I met a beautiful girl my same age from

a nearby village. Her name was Penelope.

Her hair was long, falling to her waist, amber tendrils capturing the rays of the sun. I was mesmerized by her, and fell completely in love. And, I knew that no tragedy, no misfortune, no war or cruelty of the Fates would ever keep us apart.

We married a year later, and after another year we had a son, Telemachus. And for three years, my life was bliss.

I would arise at dawn and convene with my fellow workers—my brothers—in the fields to till the soil and urge Mother Earth to give birth from the land. My brothers loved me, and would playfully jab me with a hoe, and, ignoring my lineage, call me No Man—a nobody with a hoe in his hand. But they knew at the end of the day that my toil produced twice the crop as theirs.

Upon sunset, I would return home, to my wife and son; and, although exhausted, I was happy as we embraced as a family.

My countrymen, in the other kingdoms, were, alas, not content with love of home and family.

They had yearned to sack the great walled kingdom of Troy for generations. Troy—impenetrable Troy, shielded by walls higher than Mount Olympus and thicker than the legs of Colossus.

We Greeks waited so patiently until our patience grew thin, like weathered papyrus. We waited for an excuse—a rationale—to lay the noble city under siege, kill their men, enslave their women and children and plunder their land and wealth.

And, finally, that excuse arrived in the form of a woman. That woman. The woman who launched a thousand ships."

CHAPTER XX

I looked upon him, contemptuous and amused. Cassandra had often spoken to me in dreams of the guile of the wily king of Ithaca. Now I could hear first-hand from the architect of Troy's destruction his version of history, filtered through the prism of his looming death.

"Her name was Helen," he continued. "The nubile wife of Menelaus, king from the house of Atreus. Her beauty reflected her purported lineage from the gods, and all of the kings of all of the kingdoms of Greece swore to protect her.

There was a handsome young man, beautiful as a woman, but sinewy and virile as the prince that he was. His name was Paris, son of Priam, king of Troy.

Although he was without peer with arrow and bow, he was essentially a coward, despised by his father, who loved and respected Paris' older brother, the brave and noble Hector.

Oh Paris, such a callow, superficial young man! He could have ruled the world and saved his family and its kingdom from destruction. But he betrayed all that was noble and honorable for a woman; one as callow as he—a woman of such ethereal beauty that her own treachery belied her whoredom."

I stared down upon him. I could not help but to smile. I knew beforehand all that he spoke. Odysseus, Athena's fair-haired child. Did she come to him in his dreams, as Cassandra came to me in mine?

Tragic Cassandra—hated and ignored. I could never hate or ignore her.

She told me everything about the king of Ithaca. The wandering soul yearning to go back home to his wife and son. The reluctant warrior, averse to notions of conquest and honor. My kindred spirit? My brother?

But what of the rest? The deceiver—the destroyer of Troy? His story was supported by Cassandra's dream whispers. But why did she not whisper of his violence toward my children? Did she wish to spare me grief? Or perhaps even the greatest seeress cannot see everything.

He was not finished with his desperate speech. Someone with his gift of deception cannot speak the truth forever.

I waited with joyous anticipation for that moment when he would revert to his true nature, and spin a web of lies. And when his own noose was secured around his neck, I would respond.

"I was always more of a farmer than a king or a warrior," he continued. "I loved plowing the fields, coaxing the black fertile soil to yield to the plow's blades from above and the force of life from below. I was humbled by Earth, the mother. The land beneath my feet was not truly my kingdom or domain. I, in fact, was a subject of the land.

This was all I truly wanted; to embrace the land, my son, and the true goddess in my life, my wife Penelope."

I tried to maintain a straight face as he spoke—I tried heroically. But I could feel the corners of my mouth rising involuntarily with derision. All he wanted in life was to be a dirt farmer, watching life bubble up from the ground, then receive the reward of his toils in the embrace of his adoring wife and son.

And what of his quiet lusts and ambitions? What of his complicity in the devastation of Troy and the small vulnerable allies of the great city nation? What of the invention and architecture of the great wooden horse, the horrible monument to deceit and death?

I bit my tongue as he continued. Let him reinvent himself and tighten the noose. It was actually amusing watching his mental cogs grind with desperation. I could see right through him. One powerful eye is superior to two which are blurred by self-delusion.

"One day," he continued, "I was tilling a swath of land that was incongruously adjacent to my island's sandy beach. It was rich, fertile soil steps from the sterile shore. And, as I plowed, a small group of men approached me. They were not of my kingdom, but they were Greeks.

They were a contingent of war emissaries, sent by King Menelaus, the cuckolded husband of Helen. Helen was complicit in her seduction by Paris, but this reality was reinvented as a kidnapping.

The emissaries had one purpose: to assemble all of the Achean kings in absolute solidarity to wage war on Troy. I knew—I knew by my wiles that this adventure of war upon a people who had never done harm to me, my family or my kingdom was self-destructive folly. Waging a war because of a woman's infidelity? Surely a more credible excuse could be fabricated. I saw this unjust adventure as insane at face value. I decided I would demur from the insanity by behaving in a manner they would construe as insane.

I ignored their entreaties, their stupid arguments of loyalty and glory, and began to plow beyond the soil onto the sandy beach, tossing salt into the plow's furrows where a sane man would toss seed. Surely they would conclude I was mad, and a lunatic on a mission is far more a liability than an asset.

They observed me plowing the sand. I stared blankly toward the sea, careful not to betray my deceit with facial expression.

But, alas, their leader could see my ruse.

He spoke in whispers to his comrades, and three of them departed in haste. What might they be up to, I mused?

Within minutes, the three returned, with my squalling son Telemachus in tow.

Gently, they placed my son in the path of my plow.

A truly mad man would plow over the tiny infant; a mad man who did not know the difference between sand and soil, seed from salt.

I stopped my plowing and ran to my crying son, and they knew that I was as sane as they—and as the years went on, perhaps I was the sanest of all—sane enough to abandon my family and fight in a war I found morally reprehensible; sane enough to feign respect and loyalty to men I despised and sane enough to kill men, women and children who had done me no harm. The worst atrocities in the world are committed by sane, normal men and I had acquiesced to become one of them."

The man was absolutely magnificent. His persuasive powers were nearly hypnotic. If not for my considerable experience as a victim of the art of deceit and, in all modesty, my all-consuming eye, I may have been seduced by this trickster—this master of lies.

And yet, the words he spoke were not that far adrift from the whispered narrative from Cassandra. Still, my instincts warned of treachery, regardless of what he might say.

But perhaps there was more—perhaps there were softer whispers Cassandra breathed into my ear which fell silent.

Truth and lies. Are either absolute? Perhaps there are concurrent truths, separated by contradiction. Perhaps circumstances can mitigate the truth, just as circumstances can dilute the motives of men. Indeed, I would argue that all motives are mixed.

I have no doubt that brave, conflicted Odysseus loved his wife and son. Nor do I doubt he despised the power-maddened kings and chieftains of the Greeks, who became frenzied when presented with an excuse to plunder Troy.

But I also have no doubt that his dark heart grew darker when presented with the opportunity to take and conquer—to revel in the lust of victory.

Ah, yes—Odysseus, the reluctant warrior. The faithful husband and devoted father who placed duty and loyalty to the state above the interests of his own family. Odysseus, not the strongest or fiercest of the Greeks, but the one with the greatest guile. Neither Agamemnon nor Menelaus, Ajax, or Achilles himself, could break through the impenetrable walls of Troy and bring Priam, Troy's great king, to his knees. Oh, how sweet it must have been to see Priam on his knees, begging for mercy for his family.

For ten years the Greeks recoiled from Troy's defenses, until finally the unimposing farmer/king, content with honest toil and love of family, tore great
Troy asunder with deceit and treachery in the guise of a gift horse.

I reached out before he could blink an eye, and picked him up. Oh, the indignity of such a proud man, kicking and flailing in my grasp. Oh, so delicious, the change in his expression. For a brief moment, he actually believed he had the upper hand.

As he kicked and thrashed, I took a small bite out of his thigh. A mere nibble—a love bite, if you will. He screamed— very much, I imagined, as his countless victims screamed.

How did his men perceive his panicked convulsions? Did they abandon all hope as he was diminished in their eyes? Or had they already abandoned hope, and just wished for an end, a drawn curtain bringing darkness to the final act?

The great king's breath was labored as I sat him down, his

chest heaving like a lamb's in her death throes.

He regained some composure. Then he spoke.

"Lord Polyphemus, I am a proud man, but I now concede defeat. You are bent on killing us all. But I have a final entreaty.

The wine I had offered earlier, I offer again. And now, proud king and man that I am, I find myself on my knees begging.

Please accept these goatskins of wine, no longer a gift, but as a desperate bargain. In exchange for this wine—wine coveted by the gods themselves—I beg that you not spare us, but kill us quickly and end our horror and suffering."

CHAPTER XXI

I would be deceitful myself if I said I was not intrigued by this highly touted wine. Was it a trick? Did he mix the wine with poison when I was out with my flock? To what avail? Whether they killed me with poison, or drew their swords and plunged them into my heart as I slept, they would still be trapped and die a slow death.

What if it were true? What if the wine proved headier and more delicious than even my own, renowned throughout my island? Even liars blunder, and sometimes speak the truth.

Perhaps he was truly resigned—a defeated soul who simply wanted oblivion, sooner, rather than later.

CHAPTER XXII

The goatskin was large and heavy, and the donor of the great gift, the brave and wily king of Ithaca, was showing his fatigue. The many years of war and wandering had taken their toll, and, in all modesty, his few days as my guest were less than rejuvenating. His arms trembled as he stretched upward, and for a moment I toyed with him, lingering before I reached down to accept the offering. Should I humiliate him before his men, and allow gravity to take its toll—to stare down upon him until his will and endurance failed, and the precious gift fell upon the cold stones and exploded blood red upon his feet?

But mercy and curiosity got the better of me—or at least curiosity—and I magnanimously reached down and relieved him of his great burden.

Opening the goatskin, I took a whiff of its ruby contents, and was taken aback.

The wine's bouquet was different from any I had before experienced. It was robust and bold, and as I tipped the goatskin back and forth, the wine rolled with an odd lethargy, its thick viscosity suggesting congealed blood.

I raised the goatskin to my lips, then stopped, my brow furrowed in mock consternation.

"Never drink on an empty stomach!" I bellowed.

Setting the goatskin aside, I grabbed two Greeks by the scruff of their necks, and raised them above my head. Oh, the delicious expression on their king's face—their "Noman" leader. He was so near and yet so far.

"The atmosphere in my home has grown much too somber—we need to lighten the mood!"

With that I began to twist and turn the guests in my grasp, manipulating them like marionettes as they danced in the air, thrashing about in a pas de deux dance macabre.

"Music—we must have music!" I shouted. "There has been so much death and dismay in my home these past few days—let's change the mood to one which is festive and jolly!"

They looked upon me, dumbstruck. How should one respond when the world has been overridden by the absurd and the irrational? Should one resist and try to reclaim order, or, at some point, simply surrender and flow with the chaos?

"Music, I screamed. "Every dance requires music."

My demeanor soured, and showed in my face. "If I hear no music, I fear I may go a bit mad."

As if responding to a lunatic conductor, they broke out in song! A literal Greek chorus, on note and in perfect harmony. Oh such fun—and I had yet drunk a single drop of the greatest of all wines—a wine of such perfection that the gods themselves would clash and clamor for one small sip.

They sang with perfect pitch and total conviction. They sang because singing reconnected them with earlier times— times when there was some semblance of rationality within reality, and reasonable causes resulted in reasonable effects. They sang, trapped within a cavern that loomed increasingly as a tomb. They sang for their lives—they sang for their sanity.

They sang because they could not conceive of what might happen if they were silent.

My delightful marionettes began to dance in sync with their comrades' wonderful tunes. Oh, such precise rhythm! It was almost as if the little devils had foreseen that this time would come and had rehearsed to perfection.

But how long could they sustain, I wondered? Who would falter first—the chorus, the dancing marionettes, or the puppet master whose arms were beginning to cramp from fatigue? I was not sure who would flinch first—but I knew my own will—I knew who would flinch last.

One member of the chorus began to miss notes, his hoarse voice cracking. I looked directly into his eyes, and he looked back into my immense eye—my death orb where demons swam with the absurd.

His eyes initially displayed terror, then calm as his mind

took flight.

There was a brief moment of stillness and quiet. The chorus was silent, my marionettes limp. My arms, exhausted, relaxed and lowered. Then, I raised my dangling dancers to my sides and bashed their skulls together while smiling at my weary guests.

Goodness! What has become of my sense of finesse? Their heads exploded, like melons dropped from the lofty heights of Olympus. Just in time for dinner.

And then I began to eat, voraciously, as one who is starving and protein-deficient. They were delicious. I regretted not having gotten to know them better. Had I known their names, I would have sent off letters to their parents, thanking them for providing me such a delectable meal.

As I devoured my dinner, through the corner of my eye, I looked at him. The pillager of Troy; the murderer of my children—the great and wily king of Ithaca—Odysseus.

Then, I paused and looked directly at him.

He was radiant. I saw an illuminated purity, like sunlight through stained glass.

I saw hatred, pure and without adulteration; unconditional hatred, all consuming, obsessed and without restraint.

CHAPTER XXIII

My belch was loud and vulgar. "Excuse me—pardon me please!" I declared, knowing full well my entreaty would not be taken seriously—nor should it be.

"Forgive me—please forgive my appalling manners. Quite sadly, one of the consequences of being a reclusive bachelor is an insensitivity to proper etiquette.

Perhaps—perhaps now that my appetite has been sated, an imbibement may restore me to my natural conviviality."

And that being said, I reached for the goatskin.

I took a small, tentative sip.

Can wine be truly seductive, as a woman would be seductive? The thick fluid clung to my lips, then descended slowly down my gullet, caressing and teasing. Never had I tasted such wine.

Within seconds, my perception had changed. I became relaxed—less aggressive. Was the wine adulterated? Perhaps my cunning guest put the hypnotic fruit of the lotus eaters into the already heady wine—or had Athena, the wily king of Ithaca's unfaltering benefactress, woven a spell into the blood-red brew—a spell designed for my destruction?

I raised the goatskin back to my mouth, and drank again. This time, I guzzled without reservation.

I had never imagined a wine could be both delicious and disarming. I drank again and gulped, not caring about the consequences of inebriation.

What was happening? I felt almost lethargic with tranquility. I felt unburdened and congenial.

I smiled widely as I looked down upon the donor of the wonderful gift. I seemed to know him. What was his name again?

So strange. Who are these men? Are they my friends? My memory was frozen by the strange elixir.

"Sir, I am indebted to you for this wonderful offering. Please—tell me again—where are you from and what is your name?"

He smiled. Had I retained even a modicum of sobriety I would have seen the triumphal glimmer in his eyes and the soft, gleeful curving at the corners of his lips.

"I come from the island of Ithaca, where I am most affectionately known as Noman."

Noman—I had heard that name before. Noman—the noble farmer/king who wanted nothing more than to be a man of the earth—a man who loved his family and despised war and empire.

From whose lips had I heard of this man? My memory was becoming blissfully fogged.

There was another man who had spoken to me of this Noman. Who was he? His name, teasing my palette; Ody . . . Odes . . . Od . . .?

I lifted the goatskin again, and drank. And then, the thoughts and concerns from seconds ago melted into oblivion.

I drank again from the goatskin. My memory was vacillating. I looked at him again. Of course—the fog lifted momentarily. I knew who he was. That little Greek bastard.

The wine exceeded his description. Yes—even the greatest of deceivers falter, and truth tumbles reluctantly from their lips, and sometimes truth itself can be deceitful by virtue of understatement.

I looked up at the jagged ceiling of my cave home—my sanctuary and lair. The grey dead rocks and stalactites swirled, and gained color.

Was I looking through and beyond the lifeless rocks? I seemed to be transfixed by a hypnotic kaleidoscope, a celestial tapestry of heaven.

I was insatiable for more. I reached for the goatskin. Where was it? Had I forgotten where I had placed it, or had the little trickster shit moved it, in order to toy with and torment me? What was his name? It seemed to have changed. Moments, hours, eons ago it was Od . . . Odalisque? No, it was something like that. Oddity—no, perhaps Ordinariness? No—that's it—not with an O, but an N. No—Noman. Noman had given and now he has taken away.

Where was that goatskin? When I find it, I will drink to the final drop. And then I will have Noman for dessert.

CHAPTER XXIV

I felt a pleasant giddiness as my knees buckled and my vision blurred. I sat down upon my stone chair and regained my wits.

Things had changed.

It seemed that, moments earlier, I was in complete control. The deck was stacked and I held all the cards. Now, my hand was empty, and my natural nemesis, that vicious little Greek thorn, was gaining the upper hand.

But should I not care more than I do?

The wine, the magnificent wine, made me lower my guard. But this did not deter me from wanting more.

My eye scanned the floor, through an inebriated haze. That wine; Dionysus himself would betray the greater gods for a single drop. Where was it?

There it was—right beneath my feet! Sometimes we assume that the object we most desire is farthest from our reach—a fallacy. It may be so close that it is overlooked until we stumble upon it, and trip into self-destruction.

Consequences were no longer relevant. The wine induced euphoria was all that mattered.

I lifted the goatskin to my mouth, and drank.

The stalactites from above reached down, caressing me like loving hands from lofty Olympus. Why was I not suspicious? Love raining down upon me from the gods?

Wrath and chaos were the elements most expected to fall from above; especially for me.

CHAPTER XXV

Was I lost? I looked about, and my own home appeared other-worldly. Perhaps another tip of the goatskin would clear my vision.

My next swallow was voracious.

The world spun, turning like a top, but I felt no nausea; it was pleasant and liberating. With each turn there was greater harmony. Where had all of my bitterness and hatred come from?

I could not hold thoughts for more than an instant. Where was I? Was I drunk? What would my children think of me? Where were my children?

My eye began to droop, but I could still see clearly. Who were these little men, scattered before me? They looked upon me, and contracted, drawing together around their leader. Who are they?

Ah! This brew is a teasing one. I fall back and forth, between clouded stupor and stark lucidity.

I know exactly who they are. Deceivers—murderers! And you are the foulest of them all—you—Odysseus!

I looked at him. His lips undulated, serpentine, cruel. His lips, like vipers, writhed with death.

They sensed the tables were turning, the bitch Fates shuffling their lots. Their once-fearful countenances were changing before my eye. Was this their expression—this obscene leer—that they displayed when war wearied Priam, too exhausted to think critically and too hateful of his Cassandra to heed her warning, flung open the gates of Troy and bid welcome to death and genocide in the form of an absurd wooden horse?

The blur again—the muddled thoughts of drunkenness had returned.

I looked about, my eye searching for my children. There they were, huddled in a shadowy corner. They appeared calm and content. If they were calm and content, then should I not feel the same? These little men before me—had I been too harsh? Had I reacted too swiftly to their transgressions? After all, there are two points of view; and with the involvement of the meddling gods, the viewpoints may be infinite.

CHAPTER XXVI

Sleep—the lid over my eye became ponderous. Sleep; I must sleep.

And what might befall me if I slept? What if the little men—my uninvited guests—grew closer in unison and murdered me?

It would be a suicide pact.

They would die slowly, ultimately beating their hands to a pulp against the immovable rock sealing my home and their fate.

I looked upon their leader through an unfocused eye. Was he suicidal? No—he had weathered ten years of fighting an absurd war—a war in which he did not believe, but was nonetheless the one who delivered the coup de grace. He had prevailed through storms and vortexes; through sirens, temptresses and serpents.

This was not a man resigned and defeated. This was a survivor; a survivor with a scheme.

As sleep beckoned and darkness neared, I reflected.

All of my life I had dealt with schemes. Some were my own, but not all. Lovers, rivals—the gods themselves had schemed against me. Yes, the gods themselves.

And what if the strutting little bantam cock with his lies and his heady wine were scheming against me?

What if? Of course he is.

I lay down, the feathery arms of sleep embracing and seductive. And then, I was covered by a silken blanket of darkness.

CHAPTER XXVII

The state of sleep is far more profound than rest or slumber. Sleep is a god, whose brother is death.

I had fallen into the deepest level of sleep in my life. A sleep so deep that death was tempted to usurp his brother's authority and wrap me in his dark arms and pull me down into the realm of tormented souls.

Tormented souls? Hades and hell have no monopoly on torment. For those of us who have been truly wretched—those of us who are members of the aristocracy of torment and suffering—the idea that death and damnation propel us into a state more horrific than life is tenuous. Death and damnation may be anticlimactic for those who have been accursed in life by both gods and men.

CHAPTER XXVIII

Did I feel burning and smell smoke, or was I falling into the inevitable nightmare that follows sleep? I have never slept soundly, until now. I have never awakened from a rejuvenating respite from the miseries of wakefulness. My sleep has always been haunted by demons and memories; by grim reminders of my lot in life. But this was a different kind of nightmare.

The horror was real this time, and would not be displaced by awakening to the sharp light of dawn.

I screamed, and bolted upright. The pain was beyond imagination.

Where was the light? I tried to rub the sleep from my eye, but there was only darkness. I stared into blackness—the blackness of the void.

The blackness of the stone blind.

CHAPTER XXIX

This time, my screams scorched my lungs and exploded through the natural echo chamber of my cave's many caverns. I stepped forward and burned my foot. I could feel it was a stake, torched on one end. They had driven it into my eye.

I felt the blood ooze from my eye. It was thick and salty as it pooled on my lips. I choked on the acrid stench of burnt flesh.

I began to lunge and flail, wildly at first. Then, my wits were gathered, and a peculiar calm beset me.

My lunging became controlled, my flailing methodical. In the vast blackness, I could see the contours of my cave with the vision of memory. I felt the sides of the cave nearest to me for starting point orientation. My other senses had already grown more acute.

I heard steps from outside. Not the frantic pattering of little Greek vermin, but the heavy footfalls of my brethren— my fellow cyclopses.

We cyclopses are a solitary race, and I the most solitary of all. But if attacked, we band together in solidarity.

From beyond the great stone, sealing the entrance to my home, I heard my brethrens' voices.

"Polyphemus—Polyphemus, are you not well? Are you in danger? Your screams have awakened us and shaken our entire island. Talk to us—tell us what is wrong."

It was the voice of Caltumulus, my closest neighbor. I could hear him speaking with others—Harluthemus and

Merlomulus, I guessed, who were his brothers.

"Caltumulus—help me! Intruders have entered my home. Vicious Greek intruders. Thirteen in all—or, less now—I think eight, or perhaps seven."

I could hear soft laughter from the other side. What did the laughter mean? There was an undercurrent of sarcasm and skepticism to their mirth.

"And what have these dozen, or seven, or eight Greeks done to you, oh brother Polyphemus?" replied Caltumulus. "You are the strongest of us all. You should prevail easily over a mere dozen Greeks—more easily yet over eight—or was it seven?"

My stomach churned as if the Greeks inside my belly had taken up arms and were attacking me from within. Was I to be mocked and abandoned by my own kind?

"Listen to me, brother cyclops. The leader of this murderous band of pirates has deceived me. He has murdered my most favored children and when I sought vengeance, he plied me with wine as a tribute and a bribe. But oh, no ordinary wine—wine that is more potent than that drunk by the gods—wine cursed by sorceresses. And when I succumbed to this evil brew and fell into a sleep deeper than my father's watery kingdom, this treacherous Greek blinded me with a burning stake."

There was silence from the other side—silence, the duration of which was difficult to measure in the blackened void. Then, he spoke.

"Tell us, Polyphemus, who did this to you, and we will set our shoulders to the mighty stone and tear your tormentor limb from limb. What is the name of the man who did this to you?"

If only I could see the little bastard, palsied with terror as he awaited his fate.

But the wine—the wicked wine still had a grip on my memory. His name. Was it Ody . . . Odeus? Ossid . . . no. He had told me his name himself. Yes—now I remembered.

"It was Noman," I thundered. Noman has blinded me!"

The raucous laughter from the other side struck me like an Olympian bolt. The shock had restored my sobriety and memory. How could I have not seen the clever deception? All along he was several steps ahead of me. Wily Odysseus, king of Ithaca—but his countrymen toiling in the fields knew him as humble Noman. I had believed his finely woven tale.

But before I could explain, the taunting derision boomed from outside.

"Drunken fool!" Caltumulus bellowed. "You have awakened us from our precious sleep because you've guzzled one flagon too many. Wine better than that drunk by the gods? Cheap wine will cloud your brain just as well as the gods' favorite brew if you drink enough of it. No man has harmed you—no man at all. Stagger back to your crib and let rosy-fingered dawn melt the demons of your drunken nightmare!"

I tried to scream, to call them back and tell them the true name of my enemy, but the words formed too slowly. Their howling laughter grew faint as they sauntered away, and then there was silence.

CHAPTER XXX

The wine's grasp loosened as the sun ascended, casting out the darkness—but not my darkness. I could feel the sunlight warming the cold stones of my cave. My cave—no longer my home, but a hole in the earth, dark and without hope.

And what now? What now?

"Noman," I spoke. "Noman—wily Odysseus. My head is clearing, and I remember your true name, king of Ithaca."

I dropped upon a stone, exhausted, and stared at the void.

"Look upon me Odysseus. Do you take pride and pleasure in what you have wrought? I am broken and blind and my dearest children are dead. I am alone in the universe, abandoned and despised by both gods and men. Share with me your triumph as you revel in victory. We are brothers now, rotting in the same tomb. Speak to me, O Great Odysseus."

There was silence. I was already adjusting to my fate. I could measure time by
the number and count of my breaths.

After eight breaths, I heard the sounds of steps approaching me. And I knew it was him. I could smell him. His scent was different from the others; it was unique. He smelled of death and treachery.

And then he spoke.

CHAPTER XXXI

"You misjudge me, Polyphemus. I take no joy or pride in killing, or in inflicting suffering. Circumstances drive destiny, and the tampering by the Fates into the lives of men makes free will tenuous.

I look upon you now, and feel no satisfaction in revenge, for indeed your blinding was not an act of vengeance. It was a desperate act of self-preservation, for had my men and I remained passive, or tried to reason with you, we all would have wound up in your belly in order to appease your insatiable hatred.

One can argue, Polyphemus, that we are both monsters, if not in whole, then in part; just as all of our respective races— man and cyclops—are monsters, struggling within ourselves to transcend our basic nature. But the gods and our base instincts make this struggle precarious—as precarious as the labor of Sisyphus, rolling the stone uphill, pitted against both gravity and the gods' eternal cruelty.

It is more a curse than a blessing to be a leader. To have power over the fate of other men is to usurp and infuriate the Fates themselves. Regardless of the leader's decision, there will be consequences."

I was blind, but I could see. Truth has neither form nor color. My nemesis—my pre-destined arch enemy stood before me, delivering a speech that fell somewhere between a rationalization and a mea culpa. But his words inspired more skepticism than understanding. Was he so inherently connected to me that I could look him in the eye and know him, even though my own eye was blinded?

"Let me repeat what I've said before, Polyphemus, for the truth bears repeating.

I never wanted to be a king, but I was born a prince. My father was king of Ithaca, but, who was his father and his father's father? At some point in the past—before there were kings, I believe my forbearers were farmers, as my own hands more naturally gripped the handles of the plow than the handle of the sword. The smell and sensation of black fertile soil under my feet gave meaning to my life; far more than the stench of scorched earth reeking with death, which made me believe that life had no meaning at all.

The goal of war—victory? Glory? Or perhaps merely power. Oh, what amusement we must provide the gods when they look down and see men, like ants, destroying one another's ant hills. In the end, all for naught.

I ply my wiles when I must—but I swear to you I speak only truth in this moment.

You and I, Polyphemus, are like cursed brothers. You have always loved a woman you have never seen in the flesh—Cassandra. I too have loved her. I would see her from afar, standing on Troy's tallest walls, staring down at the madness; alone and beautiful. I wanted to take her away, take her far away where her curse would be lifted and she could find love and peace.

We are all cursed, with or without the gods. We are born to suffer. And now, I am weary of body and soul, and I just want to go home."

CHAPTER XXXII

To go home. How wonderful it must be to have a home where one can return to loved ones and to the simpler ways of the past. The mere thought that home awaits the weary wanderer would give hope, even if it is an illusion.

I am home. I have no place else to go. I am home and there is no hope.

My eye has been gouged and burnt to cinder. And yet, I still see—or perhaps dream that I see. The mind's eye transcends blindness.

Am I grasping at straws? Think of the blackness of sleep. The void of sleep is punctuated by dreams. And within these dreams, when sleep is deepest, we have lucid visions, though our eyes are tightly closed.

In the blackness, images begin to form. Do I see? Or do I see only memories?

I see a man joined at the waist to a horse. He is as close to a loving father as I will ever know.

I see a merry goat man with flute in hand. Would I have ever known joy if not for him?

I see a beautiful young woman with madness in her eyes. I

see her, but I have no eye.

Oh, Cassandra, reach for me below the pond's surface and pull me away from the horror that is my life.

CHAPTER XXXIII

Already, my other senses are heightened, to the point of intrusion. I hear the trampling of my guests' feet as if elephants were stampeding, but I know it is in reality a soft patter of men trying to suffocate their footfalls. I hear them breathe—I swear I can even hear them sweat.

I smell them. I smell their breath, their fear; I smell the stench of their hatred, permeating like foul smoke wafting through my nostrils.

I reach out and hear them scuttle. I can feel their rank flesh, goose-bumped with terror, though I have not touched them.

But soon I will, and then I will taste them, and their meat will be sweeter than before—tender and juicy like ambrosia.

But unlike before, I will not kill them before I dine.

I will eat them alive, and chew slowly.

CHAPTER XXXIV

I hear. A voice? Do I hear from my Grecian guests? No—it is another sound. I hear a cry—a plea. It is my children, beckoning to me. They are hungry and thirsty. They have been distracted from their natural routine of grazing in the sunlight, beyond the dank shelter of the cave. They need to be guided to the lush pastures and clean water of the streams beyond the dark cold womb of rock where I keep and protect them.

But what of my guests? Were I to push the stone away from the entry, they would dash madly toward the daylight, depriving me of revenge—to say nothing of at least a few more tasty meals.

My children must be patient a bit longer as I shut my eye in order to visualize the possibilities.

CHAPTER XXXV

I see her. I see her face looking down upon me through a glassy film of water.

I feel. I am floating beneath a pond, but I can breathe.

Her eyes, large and dark, reflect the sorrow of the world. I see the heavens in her eyes. The stars are tears, frozen in time.

I reach up toward her and our fingertips touch. And then, something passes between us.

I know I am not alone. Her pain and mine blend, and the placid water sways. She has always known me, just as I have always known her.

I am not alone. Nor are you, Cassandra.

CHAPTER XXXVI

I must invent a way by which I can lead my children from the cave, safely and without allowing my guests to escape. But I am interrupted by distracting visions.

If I open my eye, the visions will escape, to be swallowed by the light. My eyelid is clenched tight.

I see a goddess. She is fierce, but beautiful. She is wise, but warlike. She is Athena.

They say her father is Zeus, and she was spawned without a mother. To be the daughter of the most powerful of gods is a pedigree with which to be reckoned. To be powerful and feminine in a world where gods rule supreme and goddesses are subordinate is a precarious act of balance.

I see her with total clarity. I see her, hovering over

Cassandra like a grey eyed dream cloud.

I see her providing Cassandra with protection and solace. Cassandra, in her worst moments, looks up to the sky and sees Athena. The goddess whispers, and Cassandra knows she is not alone. She has Athena—and she has me. But what good am I?

Help me, goddess Athena. Help me to help Cassandra.

The bitch Fates have spun doom for Cassandra—and they are independent of powerful goddesses and blind brutes alike.

But, you are the daughter of Zeus.

CHAPTER XXXVII

I see a shape in the dark. Large, looming, casting a death shadow beneath the moon's cold glow.

I stare at the shape and it slowly gains form and delineation. Its surface assumes curves and angles. It appears alive. It appears to be a creature.

I stare into the inky void and the shape flows into focus.

I see a horse.

I see a giant wooden horse. I can hear. I can hear sounds from within the horse. They are the sounds of men, whispering of their plot. The plot to defeat Troy.

I hear the whispering, and I hear his whispering above the others. I hear the voice of Odysseus. He is weary and has devised a plan to end the madness of the endless war. The folly of Priam and the fall of Troy. A hollow horse containing a genius of deceit. That was how it ended.

A plan of my own begins to rise. I must put an end to my own war.

CHAPTER XXXVIII

My visions within the shadowscape are interrupted by

sounds. The sounds of my children.

I had allowed myself to become distracted from their needs. They are crying for food and sunlight.

I love my children. The few, small things that are good in my life come from them. I must lead them out of the damp death chamber they share with my guests, whose mouths are watering at the sight of them. I can actually hear their mouths watering as they plot their murderous feast. But a protective shepherd must be reckoned with first—even one who is blind.

I must devise a plan where my children are released and my guests stay put.

Just as Odysseus, with his murderous wiles, is devising a plan to gain freedom and escape my revenge.

CHAPTER XXXIX

I will move the rock from the cave's entrance—but not too much. Just enough for my children to squeeze through, but too narrow for the killers to escape my grasp. My grasp. My sense of touch has increased a thousand fold. My little guests will not deceive my heightened senses.

I grasp the giant stone. How strange. Never before, when my eye had vision, did it seem so cold to my touch. Was it truly stone, or an immense block of ice? I rub my hands over its surface, remembering its contours. I will put my shoulder to the stone and move it; not too much, inch by inch, and gauge the width by sliding my hand between the stone and the opening's edge.

There! Just enough. My sense of touch is so acute I can feel the swirling dust from inside the cave. The gap is barely wide enough for my children to trundle through; but too narrow for a phalanx of Greek baby killers to join the flock and elbow their way to freedom.

I carefully push the rock back in place, and follow my children into the sunlight.

The sunlight. I feel its warmth so intensely, I can almost see it.

CHAPTER XXXX

Odysseus

I know what he is doing. Clever brute. The opening can accommodate the sheep, single file, but our girth would betray us as he swipes his immense hands over and to the sides of the flock to ensure we are not mingling to make good our escape.

The sheep waddle out, eager to greet the warmth and sustenance of the pasture. Then those gargantuan hands grasp the stone and the opening closes.

"What are we to do, King Odysseus?" asks one of my comrades. The others, voices faltering with terror, join in, pleading with me to devise a plan—a strategy in which we can escape with our lives and sail away from this nightmare island of cyclopses.

Such a burden to be king; such high expectations. They look to me with begger's eyes for salvation.

I want to go home. All other goals and desires have long ago been extinguished. I want to hold my wife Penelope—I want to feel her warmth, smell her scent and look into her eyes. Home. I want to hold my son Telemachus in my arms. How old is he? He may be a young man now. Time has gone adrift. Do I still have a wife and son? If I ever reach home, would he know who I am and would I recognize him? Home may now be one more hostile island where I awash, unknown and unwanted.

I look upon the blinded brute, his one eye scabrous in the center of his forehead. He believes I hate him, just as he hates me. But I am tired, in body and spirit. Hatred without vigor is like simmering water that grows cold and stagnant.

I look at him. He has been driven mad, as ultimately we all will be driven mad. He appears exhausted and pitiful, just as I would appear to him were he not blind.

I look upon the monster, and feel compassion. What thoughts are troubling his mind; what demons torment his soul? Can tears flow from a blinded eye, or has even weeping been taken away from him?

But I must reach home.

A plan—a scheme—a ruse or a plot. Whatever it may take to escape from this horrid place that makes Hades anti-climactic.

Whatever I must do to get back home and end this nightmare.

CHAPTER XXXXI

Polyphemus

How can I know that the sun is full in the sky if I am stone blind? Is it the warmth in contrast with the cold dampness of my home, where death and hatred fester like a malignant fog?

I was careful. My shoulder and hip were wedged tightly against the crack in the cave's entrance, my hand waving up and down to ensure no one but my children are exiting my lair.

The stone was pushed back in place and I looked up into the sky with blind eye and saw the sun. How?

Is the power of Helios so intense that even the blind are penetrated through dead eyes and can see the fiery brilliance?

What is the sun? What is blindness? Is seeing without an eye a madman's delusion, or a visionary's coup? Yes, a visionary, one who can see what is and what will be independent of eyes.

Cassandra has such vision, and always will, even if blinded in her defilement. If only I could be with her; to see her outside of my dreams—to protect her as she has protected me.

CHAPTER XL

Odysseus

"Gather about me, comrades—I have divined a scheme by which we shall escape."

My men circled me, so close that our sweat mingled and our breathing became one breath.

"Listen closely. He will return soon. We must go into hiding among the darkest nooks and crevices in this death hole, in case he has worked up an appetite for Greek flesh again.

I will place another goatskin of our potent wine where he will surely find it. Then, when he has drunk his fill and Morpheus drags him into deep slumber, we will ready our escape."

"How—how Odysseus," queried my men. "You saw how closely he felt above and to the sides of his flock as he squeezed them through the cave's opening."

I smiled. I suspect my smile was very much like the one that lit my face when I got the idea for the wooden horse.

"You have seen how large the rams are, and the thickness of their fleece. There are strong withies which the cyclops has on his bedding. I will remove a few and, in his drunken slumber, he should not be aware. I will then tie the rams in threes, with each of you tied beneath the middle one. When he leads his flock out to pasture, he will feel above and to the sides of the flock, but not below. I will save the largest ram for myself, and grasp the thick fleece on his underbelly. Then, when we are outside, I shall untie you and we will escape to our ships."

I smiled again. If my plan succeeded, never again would I object to the sobriquet "wily Odysseus."

CHAPTER XLI

Polyphemus

I can tell. I can tell by the sound of their bleats and by the feel of their warm bodies drawing close to me that they have fed and grazed enough and are ready to return to their shelter before the sunlight is swallowed by shadows.

But I must exercise great caution. As my children go in, my guests must not go out; they must never again see sunlight, just as they have taken the sun from me. But I must believe. If my will is strong and I believe, then there may be sight beyond the blindness.

I move the stone, slowly and with marked caution. I measure the opening's width with my hands and my mind's eye. Just wide enough for three abreast to squeeze through (alas, my children lack the discipline for single file.) If my desperate guests were to charge the opening, the panicked response from my children would be extreme, and I would be able within the tight area to easily grasp them by the scruff of their necks and twist off their heads.

No escape attempts, and inside once again with the cave well sealed, I greet my guests.

"I'm home! Did you miss me? I hope you haven't been up to mischief while I was gone—you know how strict I am!"

Did I actually hear some of them whine? How boorish of them. I have provided them free lodging and shelter from the harsh elements, and I have yet to hear a single murmur of gratitude. Who mentors these ill-mannered Greeks? With all of the teaching of philosophy and dialectics they are provided, was there not a single lesson in basic manners and etiquette?

Then, I could hear one of them shuffling forward. It was him. He had his own unique scent.

"Why, hello, Odysseus. Aren't you a sight for sore eye. Well, let me retract the sight part. Do you have something to say? I can think of "Noman" with whom I would rather speak."

He was so close I could feel the heat of his breath. Then he spoke.

"Polyphemus, I beg a final entreaty. If you eat more of us, then we few who are left will know we are doomed and have nothing to lose. We have discovered obscure nooks and cracks in which to hide where you would never find us in your blind state, and the next time you sleep, we will make sure you never wake up. And what would become of your beloved children? We will not perish in this musky tomb until we have devoured them all. Let us go. Your world has been darkened, but you still have your children. If you decide to leave with them and leave us alone to perish in the cave, at some point without a safe haven, the wolves will feast on their flesh, and in your blindness you will not be able to protect them. Cast away the stone and let us flee, or all of us—men, cyclops and sheep—will be together for eternity in the bowels of Hades."

These Greeks and their pernicious logic! The bastard can be persuasive.

By reflex, I take a step forward, and my foot bumps an object. I bend down, and lift it. I feel its round contours. Ah! It is a goatskin, undoubtedly filled with the heady wine the wily one had gifted me earlier.

I will drink the potent nectar. They will seal their own doom if they kill me in my sleep, but already a plan ferments in my mind of how I can dispatch my guests and save my children as well.

"Wily Odysseus, your power of reason is seductive, and your words cannot be ignored.

But I am exhausted. Let me drink of your potent wine, then sleep. Let me consider your proposal as I slumber. The blind can only see when they dream. Perhaps within the clarity of my dreams I will see no other outcome but the one you have described. Perhaps we've all suffered enough."

I turn around and tip the goatskin to my mouth as I walk to my bedding.

Perhaps we have all suffered enough?

You, Odysseus, could never suffer enough.

CHAPTER XLII

In the realm of dreams, the rules of reality are suspended. What goes up may not go down. Fish may talk and cats may bark. The sky may be brown with soil, and the ground billowy with velvet clouds.

In my dream, I hear a voice. The voice is like a whisper—a woman's whisper. Where is she? The voice is soft and compassionate. It seems so strange. Why?

Then I realize; I have not heard words spoken with compassion before.

Her voice is soothing, yet I know she has known great suffering. Her voice—like a balm carried on the wind. Is this what it is like for an infant to hear his mother for the first time, or to hear the adoring words of a lover? Did I once have a lover? It seems like a thousand years ago. Galatea—her loving words were illusions of lies and mockery.

The voice I hear is one I know. It is Cassandra's, and now the wind within my dream shifts, and her voice is carried away.

I walk about in my dream, and I see. There is a niche at the side of my cave where through the years I have stored items which have washed ashore from the sea. There—there it is among the other objects. The net. The fishing net which washed ashore years ago entwined with starfish and seaweed. I will roll the net up and remember its exact location so as not to stumble about when I awaken from my illuminated dream world. But wait—if I make changes to my world within my dream, will those changes disappear when I awake? No matter; I will find the net. I must find it. I will need the net—for the sake of my children. And for the fate of the Greeks.

CHAPTER XLIII

Poseidon

The race of men envy the gods. Oh, if they only knew.

The flaws and foibles of humanity are not absent from us—they are magnified. We have the same appetites, jealousies and impulses, but when we express them, the consequences are immense; volcanoes erupt, floods are unleashed and havoc is wrought for gods and men.

And we can be so whimsical and capricious. Once, I loathed the Trojans for reasons which are distant to me now. Then, one day, Athena appeared before me.

Oh, how I favored that one; fierce and beautiful, with a power and defiance unknown to the other goddesses. In spite of being my brother Zeus' daughter, I adored her.

One day, she appeared before me and pleaded to me for justice.

Cassandra, Priam's mad daughter, was given refuge within Athena's temple when Troy was defeated, and, as she clung to the goddesses' marble image, she was dragged outside and violated by the Greeks.

Athena now beseeches me for justice. Ha! I do not believe

in justice. It is a frail and fatuous concept concocted my men.

I believe in vengeance.

Athena wants revenge, not justice, visited upon all of the Greeks; even the one she has favored and assisted—the king of Ithaca, Odysseus.

She once adored the wily little ferret, but now?

Oh, how fickle we gods and goddesses be!

Now, even her fair haired child is guilty by association, though by all accounts he had sympathy for Cassandra, and held his own countrymen in contempt.

Oh, how convoluted the games of the gods can be. One slight by a mortal can make the dominoes come crashing down.

Odysseus, once her favorite, must be punished. Logicians take note: Odysseus is a Greek; Cassandra was violated by some Greeks, therefore, all Greeks must be punished—including Odysseus.

We gods are practically human in our thoughts and impulses. Or, perhaps, mortals are practically god-like.

Someday, the fallacies of gods and men will be exposed. Oh, Socrates, wherefore art thou?

CHAPTER XLIV

Athena

He is coming around. Poseidon, lord of the oceans and a third of the almighty triumvirate, is not immune to my charms and manipulations. No! I do not ply with charm and manipulation—those are the tools of that buxom, fat assed Aphrodite. I seduce with reason—with wiles.

Yes, just like Odysseus. Naughty boy! You must suffer a bit longer before returning home, my wandering darling. But you must not suffer forever.

Just as Polyphemus, Cassandra's brother of the soul and Poseidon's son, must not suffer forever.

CHAPTER XLV

Poseidon

She is so tall and straight, and moves with a graceful swagger. If mortals were as noble and powerful as she, we gods would be given a run for our money if they waged an insurrection.

But she is female—a goddess—and males, both mortal and god, are struck by her power and beauty.

She is impregnable to our vulgar advances, and is one with whom to be reckoned.

Always the gentleman—er, I mean gentle god—I have risen from my kingdom beneath the deep dark sea and meet with Pallas Athena, the wise and wrathful one, the irresistible warrior goddess, on a venue pleasanter for her.

I meet her on an island. It does not matter where the island is. It is an island of her choosing—or perhaps of her creation, clever girl that she is. An island of balmy weather and gentle tropical breezes, where the ambience is tranquil and calming. I look about, halfway expecting to see lotus eaters languishing on the beach. Then, the goddess speaks.

"My request of you is an ambitious one, Lord Poseidon."

"Lord" Poseidon? Come now, Athena. Even the mollusks and the sea horses are not that formal when they greet me," I reply. "A simple 'Poseidon, all powerful ruler of all the mighty oceans and all creatures, great and small, who dwell on and below the majestic seas' would suffice."

She smiles. Good. There is nothing like Olympian sarcasm to break the ice.

She looked upon him before speaking. He looked so

different on land, leaning into his throne, his crown pulled down unevenly over his head, creating an appearance more rakish than majestic.

Taking a deep breath, she spoke, her grey eyes looking directly into the god's face.

"Troy is now in ashes, and Cassandra is Agamemnon's favorite concubine. Menelaus is reunited with his whore, Helen, as he gloats in triumph. And Ajax, who defiled both my temple and Cassandra, struts with the arrogance of the victorious rapist."

Poseidon appeared distracted as she spoke, absent-mindedly plucking seaweed off his trident.

"Tell me, Athena, when Achilles slew the noblest of Trojans, brave Hector, did you observe from afar—or were you standing unseen at Achilles' side, stacking the deck against the purest son of Troy? And when cruel, arrogant Achilles tethered Hector's body to his chariot and dragged the fallen hero around the walls of Troy, did your heart fill with sorrow as Hector's mother Hecuba looked down from the walls and was driven mad by horror and grief?"

She felt as if slapped, and winced audibly. How could he know? He was not omniscient, as his brother Zeus claimed to be. It was true. Without her intervening hand, how would the duel have ended? If she had remained detached and left Achilles and Hector to their own devices, she knew how the war would have ended: Troy would now be standing tall and proud and the wood of a thousand ships would be rotting beneath the sea.

The god of the sea seemed to grow huge before her—or was she shrinking in stature?

"Perhaps I have expected too much from you, Goddess of Wisdom. The others—from obscure wood nymphs to Hera herself can be frightening in their whimsy and superficiality. I did not expect you to be so fickle in your loyalty and advocacy.

On a given day you sealed Hector's fate and hastened the annihilation of noble Troy. Then, the winds of whimsy blew through your pores and now you want the savage Greeks you championed to be punished. Oh, child of vain impulse— restore my belief in you—convince me I am being harsh and severe so once again I may look upon you as my favorite."

Her heart leapt and blood raced to her face.

Yes, she thought. She was a goddess—the goddess that the male deities respected the most. But now, her status—her character—was being challenged, and if she could not summon a robust rebuttal, she would be diminished and perceived as a leaner and more athletic version of Aphrodite, her despised antithesis.

She took a deep breath, and began.

"Yes, Poseidon, your words sting—they are arrows, precise and true. Just as you believe, so it is true; the foibles of humanity are magnified a thousand fold when possessed by the gods. And we gods and goddesses, just as men and women, are complex. At what point do our contradictions become hypocrisies? Had I cast my lot and favor with the Trojans, perhaps Achilles' mother, Thetis, would know the madness of grief as she watched the crows plucking the eyes from her son's corpse.

In the end, the Fates have the last laugh, regardless of the choices of gods and mortals."

Poseidon smiled and casually pointed his trident toward the sea. The calm was broken as huge waves battered the shore.

"My dear child—my wise and cajoling Athena. Perhaps my head has been softened by the endless currents and constant turmoil that pummel me in my kingdom beneath the sea.

I have long favored the Greeks—they are men of the sea and superb sailors as well as warriors. But they have shown neither respect nor compassion in victory. The scales must be balanced.

Agamemnon and his men will be swallowed by an insatiable tempest and he will lose most of his fleet. But his true torment awaits this murderer of his own daughter upon his return home. Yes, mothers are driven mad when their children are murdered—more so when the child was sacrificed by her own father.

Menelaus, far less brutal then his brother Agamemnon, shall be driven off course and nearly lost at sea before returning home.

Ajax, Cassandra's violator, shall drown, but not too quickly. His ship shall be torn asunder in the storm, and he will cling to a jagged rock in agony until it breaks and he is consumed by the vengeful sea. My vengeful sea. And Odysseus? He who is clever and the architect of wooden horses that bear the gift of doom?

He will wander most of all the Greeks, and will suffer longest, even after he reaches home."

Athena looked upon the god who was answering her prayers. Did she dare tempt the vicious Fates and ask for more?

The proud goddess fell upon her knees.

"Forgive me, Poseidon, if I beg for too much. There is another who has suffered more than all the others. He has endured cruelty and love loss. He has known only loneliness and pain—and now he has been blinded.

I beg you, mighty god, to have pity and to show mercy—and love—for one more.

I beg you to help Cassandra by helping your son—your son

Polyphemus."

CHAPTER XLVI

Athena

The sky grew dark and the waves rose and towered over the shore.

A god. He was a god, most powerful except for one.

There is a stark difference between approaching a god when he is in good humor, and when he is not. Timing is of the essence.

The world grew dark around us, reflecting the mood of the god before me.

"You speak of my son, Polyphemus? That misshapen brute who combines the worst characteristics and both gods and men.

When he was born, I refused to believe he was the product of my loins. His mother, Thoosa, tried to love him; but, alas, his grotesque form and that lone eye in the center of his forehead challenged her maternal instincts.

Since the beginning of time, all offspring of the gods have been awesome in their beauty and talent—except for one of mine—the one-eyed monster Polyphemus."

Athena listened. The rage from the god of the sea was tempered by a profound sadness.

The pounding fury of the sea began to recede and the thunder hushed.

Poseidon lowered his head. The sand around his feet grew moist as enormous tears fell from his eyes. Then, he raised his head and spoke.

"Oh my son, Polyphemus. Your form and lot in life did not result from a lack of virtue on your part. The Fates can be benevolent, or cruel, or random. A father, be he god or man, should embrace all of his children and provide protection and succor. I was shamed and repulsed by you, and you were abandoned by your own father. I have saved strangers from the flames of Hades and the icy tomb of the seas, but my own son has faced the brutal trials of life without champion or advocate.

Athena's words have opened my heart and mind. The time has come.

Your father will help you."

CHAPTER XLVII

Polyphemus

I awoke. The peculiar state of blindness. In sleep, I could see with stark lucidity; then, upon awakening, there is blackness. The irony does not escape me.

Nor, will my tormentors escape me.

I have forged a plan.

I will leave my cave without my children, moving the stone inches at a time so only I can exit, then I will push the stone back in place. I must exercise great caution as my guests will attack the smallest of opportunities.

I will tell the Greeks that I must retrieve water from the stream, and that when I return I will have an answer to Odysseus' proposal—but it will be a ruse!

I will retrieve the net and set a trap. Even in my world of darkness, my memory of my cave's entrance and its dimensions are etched in my mind; and my cleverness with my hands and my sense of touch have been enhanced a thousand-fold with my loss of sight.

I will rig the net above the cave's entrance with a pull rope. Then, when I return, I will tell Odysseus that his proposal is prudent, and upon the morrow I will let my flock out to pasture to provide distance between them and the wolves in Greek clothing, then I will open the entrance wide to allow him and his men to depart. It is reasonable they will flee en masse, then the rope will be pulled and they will be snared within the net.

Their screams will be like Calliope's music as I club them to death.

CHAPTER XLVIII

Polyphemus

I stand and face what I know is the rear of the cave where the Greeks would be huddled. Then I speak.

"Odysseus—wily king of Ithaca and persuader of blind cyclopses—approach me, so we may speak."

Odysseus rose up from the shadows and walked toward me. I could hear and smell his exhaustion and fear. His legs shook as he drew close.

"Tell me your thoughts, Polyphemus—tell me your thoughts."

And now the game of wits begins between the dueling deceivers.

"Hatred can cloud reason, wily king. My deep sleep has calmed my hate and excited my reason. Here is my proposal."

I pause, as if suddenly remembering something of importance. I reach for a water jug, but it is empty when I bring it to my lips. My brow curls in consternation.

"But first, I must retrieve water for myself and my children."

I ease the stone aside with a large goatskin in my hand— slowly; I must not tempt my guests to charge the daylight outside.

Now, I grab the net and do my handiwork. It goes quickly,

it seems. Then, I fill the goatskin with water and return, again moving the rock with heightened caution. Then I address the wily one.

"Today, eat your fill of my cheese and quench your thirst with my milk to regain your strength. You may rest without fear. I am groggy from your heady wine, and I too need rest. Tonight, I will sleep sober, so I may be clear headed upon the morrow. Then, I will take my children out to pasture, a good distance from the cave for my peace of mind. Then, I will return and push the stone away, and you will regain your freedom—and I, my darkened solitude."

CHAPTER XLIX

Odysseus

I listen. Without deep examination of his words, I can reasonably assume he lies. Polyphemus is mad, but the mad can scheme with clear reason.

He is treacherous. He is treacherous because he is obsessed with revenge.

I, too, am treacherous—but for different purposes. I simply want to return home, and will use any means necessary to get there.

This monstrous eater of my comrades will soon be schooled in the art of treachery.

CHAPTER L

Odysseus

Dawn—rosy-fingered dawn—breaks through the frail darkness of the sky; so bright and fiery that even the blind must shield their eyes.

I quickly rouse my comrades. We should have started sooner, but fortunately my ungracious host is still raising the dust with his thunderous snoring.

Cyclopses are as treacherous as men. His acceptance of my proposal for declaring a tie and going our separate ways was far too quick and amiable. Not delivering the final bow in our dance of death is not within his nature. How long does it take to fetch water? When we approached his cave, (what was days but seems like eons ago), there was a stream a stone's throw from the entrance. He should have been gone minutes, but he was outside for hours. Did he falter, or lose his way because of his blindness? I doubt it. He knows every nook of his domain like the back of his hand.

No—a trap has been set. He intends to contain us somehow, in tight, inescapable confines, where even in his blindness he can dispatch us with ease.

But this does not nullify or diminish my original plan. We will exit his morbid den attached to his sheep and sprint toward our ships with the speed of Hermes.

The brute has shifted in his slumber and grunted. Soon, he will awaken.

My men and I have rehearsed our plan to the point where our movements are reflexive.

The sheep have been bound together by threes. I will grab the thick fleece of the huge ram. My men have been tethered to the underbelly of the center sheep of the bound trios.

Then, he awakens. Standing, he emits a huge yawn, then clears his throat and speaks.

CHAPTER LI

Polyphemus

"Good morning, my dear Odysseus and surviving compatriots."

What is it about early morning that has always inspired my

sarcasm? A caustic remark or two helps break up the morning phlegm.

"I hope you have slept soundly, my friends. I would imagine you are a bit ambivalent about your quality time with me. But, if nothing else, the dwindling occupant density of your quarters should have allowed more elbow room and a more relaxing slumber."

What—what did I hear? Did the wily one just swear beneath his breath?

"Noman—is that you? Oh, by the way, may I call you Odysseus? Are you ready to thank me for my hospitality and bid me adieu?"

Ah, if only I could see the hatred on his face, just as I could hear the hatred bursting through his pores.

"We are indeed ready, Polyphemus. I hope all of our lives have some salvage value. It is time—time for all of us to move on.

Go—lead your children to safe haven, then, when they are far from our clutches, return and send us on our way."

The sound of his voice whets my appetite. To truly enjoy a meal, it should be a total sensory experience. Alas, I will have to settle for four senses when I crack his skull like a nut and render his brains into a fine pate.

CHAPTER LII

Odysseus

He is moving the great stone. My men, tethered to the sheeps' underbellies, look up at me, their faces frozen in fear—and hope. They believe in me, more than they believe in Fates or gods.

The entrance is opened. The cyclops waves his gigantic hands over the backs of his "children" as they squeeze through the opening to assure there are no passengers. Good! My plan is working. Now, I grab the large ram and grasp him by his belly's fleece with insane urgency. My grip is fierce, but I must exert care as to not grip with such frenzy as to make him baa in distress.

Daylight! The sun strikes our faces as we peer up beyond the sheeps' undersides.

Is this what the leap from embryo to infant is like when we burst forth from the womb? We are struck by a sensation, pure and life affirming. The flock is led a good distance from the cave—not as far as Polyphemus indicated, treacherous bastard—but for our purposes, far enough.

I look upon him. The bastard smiles. He believes we are still imprisoned in his cave. He is confident he has beaten us; that he has defeated me.

As he swaggers back to seal our fate, I move quickly.

I untie my men. We can see our ships, still moored where we washed ashore.

We dart toward the ships. Even Hermes could not keep our pace.

CHAPTER LIII

Polyphemus

Memory acts as vision when one is blind. My memory of my home and its environs is indelible, and I return to the cave with unfaltering haste.

My hands fall upon the stone sealing the cave. I push it aside with eager anticipation. I reach for the rope, hidden within a crag that will release the trap. Then I speak.

"Odysseus—it is time. Return to your ships and set sail for home."

Silence. There is no response. He is being cautious and

relying on stealth—yes, caution and stealth.

Then, I hear a sound, like a desperate flutter.

I pull the rope, and the net comes down.

In an instant, the club is in my hands and I begin to deliver blows with a lunatic frenzy.

"Die—die you Greek bastards—you killers of my children who lay waste to noble cities and blind sleeping giants—die—die!"

I wield the club until exhaustion makes my arms too heavy to lift. But something is wrong.

Where are their screams? Why do I not feel the crushing of bones and the splattering of entrails as I wield the club?

I fall upon my knees and run my hands over the net. There is nothing beneath it. Wait—what is this? I pick up something. Something small, warm and dead. Softly, I caress its crushed surface.

I feel wings. It is a bat. Nothing more.

The Greeks have escaped my wrath.

I lift my head and scream, but the god of the heavens is deaf and indifferent.

But what of the god of the seas?

CHAPTER LIV

Where am I? I feel lost and small. There is silence in the darkness. Am I alone? Am I all that there is in the void?

I run my hands over my face. I can feel. I feel the scars and crags beneath my beard. I touch the scab upon my eye, dry and brittle. I moan, and know I have a voice. I cannot see, but I stare at the endless sea.

It is time. Time for the end. The end of hate and hope; of suffering and longing.

Why was I ever thrust into this world? For what purpose?

There may be no purpose, or answers.

I run my hand down to my waist. I feel the talisman tied to my belt; my trophy of hair and scalp I took from a cruel and arrogant rival—Acis, the beautiful Acis. Should I have killed him? And what of Democulus? He was a monster. I could have made it fast by snapping his neck like a twig. But he reveled in inflicting suffering, just as I reveled in watching him suffer impaled upon the staff. Am I any less a monster than he? And what of the Greeks? They drove me mad by what they had done to my children—but is madness a justification for murder?

I try to feel guilt and remorse—and fail. They deserved to die—and I, no less than them.

My hand wanders across my belt, and pauses when I feel the sheath. I remove the knife, the blade razor sharp. I raise the blade and place it against the soft hollow of my neck. In but a moment all of my thoughts and pain, my nightmares and sorrowful memories will bleed into the void and all will come to an end.

And then I heard music.

The music was exotic, yet familiar.

I replaced my knife into its sheath and listened more intently. The music grew louder. I knew that music.

It was flute music. Flute music that was unique and hypnotic. Flute music that could only be played by one flautist—Pan.

The music stopped and I heard his voice.

"No, Polyphemus—the time for you to depart has not yet come.

You are blind, in despair and alone. But you are not alone. I am here. And Cassandra, in spirit if not in flesh, is here."

"Pan—is it truly you?" I reach out, extending my hand into

the void. "Touch me Pan—grasp my hand so I will know the Fates are not conspiring with my imagination to further torment me with figments."

I feel his touch, and know it is Pan—my friend Pan. Suddenly, the void is not so empty or so dark.

"What do I do, Pan? I am lost. There is no more meaning in my life than there is meaning in the world. Why—why should I not end the agony that has been endless?"

There was a brief riff of flute music, then, Pan replied.

"If life has no meaning, then you must create your own meaning. Forge value from the flames that have immolated your body and spirit. Plant it—force it into the ground—nurture it and make it grow.

And remember; you are not without responsibility. Without you, your children will perish. You can still love and protect them, whether you can see or not."

I hold onto Pan's hand. His touch is warm, and I am reconnected to a time when life's hardships were punctuated with music and joy. So long ago.

"Pan—play for me, Pan. I yearn to hear that magical music I first heard, it seems, so very long ago."

I hear the music. It starts, slowly, as if dripping off the flute with sadness.

Then, the tempo picks up, and the sad notes gain life and energy. I am blind, but I see the music. As Pan plays faster, I see colors, brilliant and pulsating. The colors grow brighter as the music builds momentum. I feel the music as its energy begins coursing through my blood.

The music becomes louder, the rhythm bringing joy back into my heart, as it did the first time I heard it. "Play—play for me Pan; make me dance to your merry melodies—make me remember how things could have been, and forget how they really are."

The music builds, climbing high, ascending, perhaps all the way up to Olympus. If I hear the sound of thunder it will be from the gods up on high dancing upon the clouds. Then, the music stopped, and Pan spoke.

"You saw the music as I played, did you not Polyphemus? But how can one see, without an eye?

Our universe is a strange one—we think we know when the final lot has been cast by the Fates, but this is due to our arrogance. We do not know the end any more than we can remember the beginning.

But hear me on this, Polyphemus. Listen, as if Chiron himself were speaking.

Nothing is permanent. Nothing—not joy or despair, hatred or love, or, as you believe now, eternal darkness.

Never surrender. Chiron saw so many good things within you, qualities which you never allowed yourself to see. And one of those qualities he admired most was your perseverance.

I must leave you now. But as I depart, I will play my flute once more—but this time my music will be directed not to the heavens, but to the sea."

He began to play, and the music was powerful, not a joyous melody but a loud, clear clarion call.

And, as he departed, I could hear the sound of hooves upon the ground, but louder and heavier than those of a goat. No, I am sure of it, it was the sound of horse hooves, and as they grew distant I also heard a familiar sound—the sound of horse lips, making a vague fluttering sound.

Or perhaps it was just the wind.

CHAPTER LV

I walk, trance like, toward the sea. The sea, the eternal

cauldron where all life began.

The waves grow louder and my face is moistened by spray. I have reached the shore.

I fall upon my knees, exhausted and humbled. I have no eye, and yet I weep. I speak.

"Help me father. Your son begs for your help.

I did not design what I am or what I have been. Where others have known love, I have known only hurt. Am I ugly, father? I do not mean to be. I am not the sculptor of my image. A god's son should be beautiful, but I am repulsive. He should be powerful, but I am brutish.

I have known such pain and loneliness, my father. If only I could be a child again. If only I could be pure and innocent.

What have I done, father? Is a cyclops so different from a man? Should a man's suffering be proportionate to his sins?

Please, father—try to look upon me, not as a gruesome mistake or an insult from the Fates, but as a son.

A son who begs for mercy from his father."

I hear. Waves are crashing upon the shore. The wind howls, primal and fierce.

I hear the whip crack of thunder, and sense lightening drawing near.

I am struck!

I fall back upon the sand. There is a dizzy fire in my head. I hold my hands across my eye. I feel burning again, as when I was blinded.

The wind's howl becomes my own. Slowly, I remove my hands from across my eye.

There is light. I see.

I see the earth and the sky, and my father's domain, the sea.

I look into the distance, and I see ships. It is them. They have not gone far.

Am I mad, or has a hateful father's own blindness been lifted and he has finally bestowed a gift to his wretched son?

Do I see? Do I truly see? Speak to me; speak, father Poseidon. Let me know you have restored my sight and that the Fates are not tormenting me with illusion.

I hear a roar from beneath, like thunder, crackling from the bottomless depths.

There—just beyond the shore. A geyser erupts from the sea, a dark spinning monolith, rising to the sky, striking the heavens.

A sign, from one god to his brother; from a father to his son.

I run toward the cliffs, my island's highest point. I climb, the sharp rocks providing footholds. I reach the top.

"Odysseus—can you hear? You are not that far off. You can hear me."

I see! I see farther than I could ever see before. I see his face. I see his eyes, as if he were standing next to me, bursting with astonishment.

"Forgive me, king of Ithaca. I have not been a proper host. You left with such haste, I did not have time to give you your going away gift. Fortunately, it is not too late."

I grab a boulder, ripping it from the stony cliff. It is enormous—as large as Odysseus' ship. My strength is absurd. I am powerful—like the son of a great god.

With a bellow, I throw the stone towards the ships. I can see his men, pulling their oars with desperation.

The gigantic boulder falls in front of the ships.

The sea explodes and creates a wave of such enormity that the ships are driven back toward shore, in the path where a jagged reef lies.

The air is curdled with the sound of screams as all ships are thrown against the rocks.

There is quiet. Then the gulls appear, pecking at the shattered timber and mangled corpses.

They have all perished. I raise my arms in triumph—but wait.

There is a survivor.

It is him—noble Odysseus, clinging to a broken mast.

I reach for another boulder, but my arms are stayed, as if Athena herself has intervened.

And then, I think of her.

"Hear me, Cassandra. Our souls are attached. You are the one I have always loved.

We have been chosen, to see and feel far more than the gods and men can ever know. Whatever happens, our love is immortal—and if not on earth, then someday in heaven we shall be together."

Then, I look down upon him again.

"Hear me, brave Odysseus. Your final lot has not yet been drawn. You will suffer more, and survive. Persevere. Someday, you will reach home—and redemption."

And for you? For all of you who may cross my path?

I am solitary by nature and distrustful of strangers. I reserve my compassion and mercy for lambs and children and all who are innocent.

And if you are nearing home and your ship is driven off course by a hurled boulder, and if your comrades disappear in a maelstrom of your own design, do not look up into the heavens for salvation or down to hell for forgiveness. I know. I scream in defiance at the absurd and fling vengeance into the abyss.

And when you sink into oblivion, do not cast blame on the Fates, gods, or treachery of others.

I, Polyphemus

You must know it is I—I am the cause of your destruction—

I, Polyphemus.

Ron Terranova is a retired real property appraiser who lives in Huntington Beach, California. He began writing at age eleven after nearly dying from a serious illness. During his recovery he fell in love with Greek mythology. The fantastic tales of gods and heroes drew him away from his illness, and impressed upon him the power of imagination and the written word.

He has had many poems published, most recently in Chiron Review, and is the author of "October Light", a collection of eclectic short stories which include the macabre, noir and absurdist genres. He also is a regular reader for Orange County Dimestories, and his flash fiction can be heard online.

www.rterranova.com

Also by REaDLips Press:

Eddy – Noreen Lace

Appalachian Alchemy – Barlow Adams

See our catalogue at <u>www.readlipspress.com</u>